THE MAYFAIR BANK JOB

THE MAYFAIR BANK JOB

Stephen Skinner

GOLDEN HOARD PRESS
2018

Published by Golden Hoard Press
P O Box 1073
Robinson Road PO
Singapore, 902123.

www.GoldenHoard.com

© Copyright 2018 Stephen Skinner
www.SSkinner.com

First Edition

All rights reserved. No part of this publication may be reproduced or utilized in any form or by any means, electronic or mechanical, including photocopying, recording, or by any information storage and retrieval system, or used in another book, without specific written permission from the author. The only exception to this being fair use in a review.

ISBN 978-0-993204265

"Teenager Ian MacPherson's passion for pop landed him bang in the middle of the Great Mayfair Bank Raid.

He was dialing a disc at the bank where he works when suddenly he found a gun at his neck.

Ian and two other night computer workers at the Davies Street branch of the Bank of America were bundled into the bank basement.

And there four armed raiders calmly carried on plundering the vault of an estimated £2,000,000 in cash and gems.

But their real prize was their haul of gems and other valuables from the deposit boxes. This is thought to be worth at least £1¾ million. And the final total could be much higher"

…it was.

- *Daily Mirror*, Saturday, April 26, 1975

CONTENTS

0	Prison	9
1	What we Found	11
2	The Bank takes a Hit	15
3	The Team	25
4	Johnny Wilde	35
5	Planning the Job	45
6	Spying the Combination	55
7	The Bank yields up its Secrets	61
8	The Vault	73
9	The Slaughter	81
10	Arrests and Grassing	93
11	Arrests and Escapes	105
12	O'Shaughnessy's Escape and Banner's Trial	115
13	The Sweet Smell of Corruption	123
14	On the Run	133
15	Trial and Sentencing	149
16	Buried Treasure	161
Glossary		174
Appendix		178

INTRODUCTION - Prison

Christ! Ten past ten. Only two minutes since I last looked. You'd think after 16 years that another 10 minutes wouldn't make any difference. I tossed the third fag end out of the car window. The noise of a bolt being pulled back reached my ears and I looked expectantly towards the gates. The prison was one hell of an institution, Victorian gothic at its very worst.

Through the small side gate a man's shoulder appeared. I realised I had actually stopped breathing. Shit! It wasn't Johnny. A warder stepped through and then stepped back again and the door closed. What the hell was going on? The door opened again almost immediately out stepped Johnny Wilde. For a moment I didn't even see him. I'd prepared myself for him looking older, but even so the way he looked took me back a bit. I slid the car into gear and eased forward sliding alongside him and the kerb.

"Get in Johnny," I said through the open car window and lent over and unlocked the passenger side. "Throw you bag in the back." What noticed most was how much slower he seemed. He didn't smile.

"How yer doing then, mate?" Plenty of time to catch up later I thought. As we moved out onto the motorway involuntarily both of our thoughts drifted back to that Spring evening in April 1975...

Chapter 1 - What we Found

None of us knew what we were about to find. Yes, it was supposed to be a good haul, maybe if we were very lucky over a million pounds: not a bad night's work, even split ten ways. What we found that night in the Bank of America in Mayfair rewrote the history books.

All I was asked to do was clean up the 'slaughter.' When you do a robbery of any kind you have got to have a place to go to divvy up, a place of safety to re-group and later disperse from, a place to carve up the spoil, a slaughter. The Great Train Robbers used Leatherslade Farm as a slaughter after the event to sort out their haul of mail bags and share it out.

My job was to clean up every trace, wipe away the prints and burn anything left over, so that not a shred of evidence remained which might connect the slaughter with the robbery or with the robbers. All the bags that were used to transport the haul, any papers, cheques or non-negotiable certificates, letters and traceable assets all had to be reduced to untraceable ashes. Such a waste, such a pity…but necessary.

The haul contained a bewildering array of items, currencies, some instantly usable, some dangerous if cashed, jewelry, Krugerrands (a much more popular form of pure gold coin investment in those days), platinum bars, banknotes in almost any currency you can imagine, share certificates, bearer bonds, option certificates and of course the inevitable dossiers of papers, even some that James Bond would have felt at home with. Being the closest American bank to the American Embassy, it was not surprising that some of the boxes belonged to the American security services, the CIA, who perhaps felt more comfortable with their papers shut up here than they would have felt in a British bank, or even their own Embassy strong-room in Grosvenor Square.

Added to which there was a mass of things which the bank's well to do customers preferred not to keep where their wives, sweethearts or staff could find them, such as whips, pornography, love letters, drugs, blue films, guns and even machine-pistols. Nobody on the team knew exactly what they were going to find. Nobody knew exactly what was hidden in all those sober faced steel boxes, not even the Bank of America.

The very area, Mayfair, smacks of money, both hereditary and new business, some ill-gotten, some hidden from the taxman or the divorced wife, some put away for a rainy day. All the safe deposit customers were almost completely certain that it was safe, safe at least from everything except inflation.

The Bank was just down the street from Claridge's Hotel, in the heart of London's wealthiest area. Being an American Bank, many of its safety deposit box owners felt it was less likely to blather about their affairs to the ever nosey Inland Revenue. These customers thought their money and their secrets were totally safe in that bank. Even if the Bank of America had gone bust, the contents of the easily identifiable steel boxes behind flush steel locker doors would still be the property of their canny owners.

Such a box was much safer than a bank account. Subsequent experience of events like the infamous BCCI scandal or the Bank of Cyprus' depositors' funds 'haircut,' has shown that a bank can freeze an account and eventually return only some fraction of it, after the liquidators have received all their expensive fees and the various investor regulatory bodies have decided who has to make up each depositors account to the statutory 80 or 90% that was on deposit. Not to mention all that undesirable publicity, and the opportunity afforded to the Inland Revenue. Far safer to keep cash in a little steel box in the bank basement, nobody's business but your own...or so they thought.

Nobody thought that on the night of Thursday 24th April, 1975, an almost perfect robbery would empty all these secrets on to the floor, and remove hundreds of these secret stashes in the space of a few short hours. This is the story of that robbery, the people who did it, and what happened to them, and the money.

The first Safe Deposit vault was opened in New York in 1865. In England, apart from the tradition of leaving valuables with goldsmiths, the first public vault, the National Safe Deposit Company, opened its doors in 1872, followed by the Chancery Lane Safe Deposit vault in 1885. Ironically Britain's first seven day a week facility was opened by the Berkeley Safe Deposit Company in 1980, in Davies Street, just a few doors down from the Bank of America's vaults.

When in November 1976 the *Sunday Times* finally told the story behind the break in to the Mayfair branch of the Bank of America, they described it at the time as "the largest bank robbery in the world." There have been bigger thefts since, such as the Brinks Mat job at Heathrow, but at that time, the Bank of America break-in in Mayfair was unique in the annals of crime.

Even now, if you convert all the really big UK robberies into today's currency, using purchasing power as the indicator, then the largest is still the Bank of America at an inflation adjusted £197 million, followed by the Knightsbridge Safety Deposit Vaults at £101 million, the Brinks Mat gold raid at Heathrow Airport at £80 million, and then the Great Train Robbery at £49 million and Lloyds Baker Street at £38 million, all adjusted to 2016 values.

But that was some way in the future. It all started one rainy day in 1974…

Chapter 2 - The Bank takes a Hit

Stewart Banner, a slight insignificant looking man with dark curly hair, who was just 26, was hired as the Bank of America's maintenance electrician in March 1974, just weeks after getting out of jail. He had completed a nine month sentence for handling stolen goods. When he later came to trial, he asked for a further thirteen offences to be taken into account, acknowledging that he had been quite 'lively' in the business of removing and reselling goods which had not been taken adequate care of by their previous owners.

He had a quiet manner, but seemed always eager to help. It was this eagerness to help which had got him into trouble with the law already, when he had helped the much more wily thief Freddie Leaf with one or two of his 'tickles.' Leaf was a very creative robber and had to a large extent done the planning, but had also allowed Banner to take the fall for many of their escapades.

Banner did not live it up like many small time criminals, nor did he spend all his days in the boozer. He lived with his parents in a quiet street in south London, just off Clapham Common. He had married, but the marriage lasted only a few months. After he got out of jail, he was doing the odd job when his brother Keith had told him that the Bank of America needed a subcontracting electrician. Banner applied, and was rather surprised when he got the job. The Bank did not think to check his references.

He was by any standard, a 'wizard' electrician, having applied himself to books on the subject, and learnt more than just routine rewiring. He could not believe his luck when the bank took him on without even cursory checks: perhaps they reasoned that as a subcontractor they did not need to subject him to the normal staff vetting procedures. In the course of his duties he had full access to the areas adjoining the vaults and to the security system, if not actually to the vaults themselves. In many ways he got to know more about the bank than its manager.

In the same week he got the job, in a pub in Wimbledon he met with some friends who were more than just politely interested in his new job. His natural inclination was to talk about the details of such things as the bank vaults, the alarm system and its security procedures with the pride of discovery. This loose talk was met with attention only occasionally punctuated by jocular suggestions as to how he could put his new found knowledge to good use. A few days later, Freddie Leaf, with whom he had 'worked' before, met with Banner in the Falcon Pub, Falcon Road, Clapham Junction and again in the Crooked Billet pub in Wimbledon, London SW19. Freddie was tall, good looking and at 36 about ten years older than Banner.

Freddie had a shock of hair which he often wore quite long. With a moustache and full beard, which he was later to sport on his travels round Europe, he looked like the archetypal hippy, but he had an inner strength that made people like Banner look up to him. Freddie very soon suggested to Banner that "the bank has a lot of money, and perhaps it's about time they parted with it."

Initially diffident about parting with really specific details, Banner began to work on a plan, drawing up a blueprint of the bank's layout, and the timing of its everyday routine and security precautions.

The bank was located in a nondescript building on the corner of Davies Street and Grosvenor Street, adjacent to the Canadian Embassy, two blocks from the US Embassy in Grosvenor Square, and one short block from Claridge's, that most discreet of top bracket London hotels. Nobody would normally give the nondescript frontage of the bank a second thought. Behind the bank a small mews, such as only London seems to have in any quantity, called Three Kings Yard, gave access to the back of the bank, and a number of other businesses who did not want tradesmen or deliveries calling at their front doors and compromising their upmarket Mayfair image.

The bank occupied three floors, the basement housed the vault, toilets and storage areas, street level provided the usual banking hall and counter facilities, and the floor above this housed the computer department. Because the bank was a branch of the huge Bank of America chain in the US it tended to stay in touch with its parent and the international markets through the day and night, with the computer running virtually round the clock. Staff from the first floor above street level would often pop in or out at change of shift, or simply to go for some light refreshments.

This meant that Banner and his friends could come and go as they wished without causing too much suspicion. The fire exit to this Yard was locked, but Banner was soon provided with a key by one of London's finest and most successful 'keymen,' Johnny Wilde. Banner was, at the behest of his friends thus able to carry out detailed tours of inspection of those 'secure' areas normally denied to him during his daylight hours on the job. At the request of Freddie Leaf and his keyman, he took all the measurements he could, and also noted down the serial numbers of the alarm system and the vault itself. For this sort of plan every detail mattered.

Johnny Wilde, who was considerably older than Banner at 51, was introduced to him by Freddie Leaf who by now was masterminding the exploratory stage planning. Freddie had one of the most fertile criminal minds in London. His main weakness, apart from pretty women, was not being able to resist a good 'tickle.' Johnny was known to his friends in the trade and in the Fulham pub where they all met as Johnny Wilde. Another name he sometimes used was the old name of the area he lived in, now called Palmers Green or Southgate. He was definitely the 'King of the Twirls' (slang for keys), and could often be found at home sitting comfortably working with different locks, until in a very short time, they clicked open in his hands. He was fascinated by the precision movements of the best locks, which rival clock mechanisms in complexity. There was very little he did not know about the inner workings of even the most complex locking mechanisms.

His friends affectionately called him Johnny 'the Bosh,' in celebration of one of his inventions which enabled him to open and start any car within seconds. With his infamous tool even the most sophisticated motors could be 'boshed' open almost faster than their owners could have started them.

The *Sunday Times*, unaware of the existence of this extraordinary device, erroneously speculated that he was called 'Johnny the Boche' because of his supposed Teutonic appearance. He was by trade a greengrocer, a usefully cash based business through which flowed some of the fruit of his key-based exploits.

Banner took Johnny into the bank on several occasions to check out the configuration of the vaults, and to secure extra copies of keys to other rooms, gradually building up a set which gave him access to most parts of the bank. On one occasion they even found crucial keys in an unlocked manager's desk, where the process of copying them was the work of a few minutes. These keys worked the locks which protected the combination locks themselves from casual access.

One evening they were both down reconnoitering the anteroom to the vault, having first taken the precaution of turning up the 'musak' which continuously played throughout the bank premises. Johnny Wilde carefully examined the twin combination locks with some bewilderment. He had never seen this type before and was unsure of the best way of tackling the job of opening the huge door.

Obviously the vault door was too large and modern to apply a combination of drilling, wedging and levering. With staff constantly upstairs, blasting with nitro or gelignite was also not an option. Using-thermal lances or a metal burning bar was not really Johnny's style, but might have served to open the huge door, given enough time. In fact the early seventies had almost seen the end of safe-cracking, as more and more money transmission was done by computer, and less by actual cash. Unfortunately for his expertise, the vault door was combination locked rather than key locked. For Johnny Wilde, there were only two choices.

Either the combination had to be secured, a difficult task as there were two separate locks, with the combinations known to separate members of staff, and not to Banner. Alternatively he had to drill into the vault door to reach the exact spot where the delicate combination mechanism was hidden, and using his incredibly light touch, move each of the tumblers out of the way, so the lock could be opened.

The time-honoured film scene of the burglar using sharply tuned ears, a stethoscope or even an amplifier to hear the tumblers fall on each turn of the dial was not an option. In reality this approach only works on very old or very cheap combination locks, which click as they fall. Such an approach is not likely to get anywhere on a modern and expensive vault door, with well-oiled precision mechanisms.

It was therefore of the greatest importance to recognise not just the manufacturer but also the model number of the safe or vault under consideration, so that the exact position of the tumblers, deep within the door, could be pinpointed.

Johnny Wilde had not seen this type of vault before, and not only were there two combination-locks to deal with, but both were themselves extremely complex, and protected in their turn by special doors which had to be opened first. Fortunately they had discovered one of the keys to these in the unlocked manager's desk on an earlier foray.

Painstakingly he unlocked the door protecting the vault door and set about taking painstakingly accurate measurements of such things as the distance from the edge of the door and the position of the circular handle which withdrew the bolts once the combination had been successfully surmounted. Johnny had brought his Vernier gauge, accurate to more than one 900ths of an inch, used by key makers for extremely precise measurements, and checked both the key he had found in the manager's draw, and the lock which would have been opened by the chief cashier's key to which they did not have access.

He also took Polaroid photos of the vault door to help him later match the exact model with the photos in the correct handbook. These handbooks, available only to the trade, were sometimes sold to 'keymen' such as Johnny Wilde (who had built up a reference library of them) by unscrupulous safe makers or locksmiths.

On the next visit Johnny, who had done his homework in the meantime, decided that on the night scheduled for the raid, small holes should be drilled an inch from the centre of each combination lock, at a precise angle. Once the mechanism chamber had been reached, Wilde planned to insert his iron 'feelers' through the holes to move each of the tumblers restraining the bolts. When the last dropped into place, the large 'ship's wheel' could be turned to simultaneously withdraw all of the restraining bolts.

Other hazards often encountered by keymen were secondary locks which closed if the vibration of a blast or the heat of a thermal lance were detected. Johnny was confident that he could coax the tumblers into position without affecting these secondary safeguards. By now the 'firm' as they had come to think of themselves, had grown with the introduction of Michael Jevons, 'Mickey' to his friends, another electrician, who was brought in as the 'bellman' or alarms expert.

Banner was not sure that he knew exactly what to do to ensure that the alarms did not either silently alert the local police station, or rather more noisily go off on the wall outside. The alarm in fact was a 'record player' type which when activated worked just like a LP player, but lowered its needle on to a specially recorded disk which would transmit a verbal message by phone line to the local police station, repeating the address and the warning of a break-in until stopped. Jevons came up with the simple but effective idea of silencing the alarm by removing the needle from the player arm, so that even if it was triggered, no message would be transmitted.

A fifth man, William Gavroche (Willy to his friends), who lived near Stewart Banner in Streatham, and whose main business interests were a local betting shop, volunteered to act as a lookout man. Willy was one of those instantly likeable villains who are always cracking jokes, always the life and soul of any party. These were the main, but by no means the last members of the 'firm.'

The planning had been meticulous. Many meetings had taken place in Wimbledon and Fulham pubs. As is the case with all such 'jobs' more people were involved in the discussions than actually went on the job. Although the participants were known to each other, the potential for grassing either before or after the raid was one of the greatest risks. The date set for the attempt was Friday 26th October 1974, in fact the whole weekend if necessary.

Leaf thought that Saturday was likely to be the safest period for the job, and suggested to Banner that he make sure that he was nowhere near the Bank over the weekend, especially on Saturday, and that he arrange to be seen by plenty of reliable friends and non-family members, so he would have a watertight alibi. The first Group Four security guard came round to the Bank at about 6 pm on Friday and would return at intervals till Saturday morning.

Between this visit on Friday evening and Saturday morning the gang turned up equipped as if to do repairs, with a full set of holdalls containing power cables, drills, electromagnetic clamps and special bits designed to pierce hardened steel. The measurements were carefully marked out on the door by Johnny Wilde, and the drill positioned at the right angle to reach the tumbler chambers. The electromagnetic clamps were turned on and the drills were positioned against the unyielding surface of the vault door. The drills were muffled as much as possible and the power to the drills was turned on after the background 'muzak' had been turned up. Two floors up, the computer staff went about their business oblivious of the activity in the vault.

The bits started to bite into the surface of the steel door. Everyone's eyes, except Willy Gavroche, who was on the ground floor and keeping a lookout, darted from the drills to the doorway and back, watching in case a straggler from the computer department should come down the steps to the vault area toilet.

The drill bits slowly turned from black to red as they overheated and lost their 'temper.' Every time they overheated they either snapped or stopped penetrating the steel plate of the door. After a few nervously ribald jokes about the need for a source of liquid to cool the bits, one of the gang broke into the drinks vending machine and started pouring can after can of ice-cold coke over the bits. They began again to bite into the steel. The men, unable to do anything but watch and wait moving uneasily round the small antechamber to the vault.

The regular replacement of failed bits began to get on everyone's nerves. As the bits heated up so did their tempers. Johnny Wilde, who would have been much more at home crafting keys to turn in locks, was accused by other members of the firm of bringing the wrong equipment. He sullenly told then to shut up. To his consternation, some of the members started pressing down hard on the drills to try and speed up the process. As the pressure was increased, the bits wobbled and were in danger of fracturing.

Suddenly Willy Gavroche, keeping lookout, saw two computer staff approaching the vault areas. He tried shouting a warning to the men around the vault door, but the noise of the drills drowned his warning. In desperation he turned off the power. Too late he realised his mistake — not only did the drills stop turning, but so did the grip of the electromagnetic clamps. The drills snapped their already overstretched bits and fell to the floor, leaving parts of the bit's length jammed in the precisely calculated and angled holes.

Silence prevailed until the two computer staff left the bank floor, then tempers flared and voices were raised. The exact alignments were now unusable, and the holes were occupied by snapped off drill bits. Trying to drill out these bits, ruined four more bits in quick succession. They stood around, each coming up with more preposterous suggestions. Johnny wanted to hit Willy Gavroche. Reluctantly they decided to give up. The raid had been a disaster. Amazingly, the staff upstairs were still totally oblivious of the goings on in the basement.

In fact the next Group Four security guard never even inspected the vault area on the three rather desultory visits that he paid to the Bank: one was at exactly 7.42 pm on Saturday evening, then just after midnight at 12.38 on the Sunday morning, and a third time at about 4.20 am on Sunday morning.

The next morning another and more thorough Group Four security guard checked thoroughly at 11.32 am, and this guard did go into the vault area. He found the debris of the raid, the broken drill bits, the coke cans and the dried residue of the coke which had been used so liberally as a coolant the night before. The smell of urine also hung in the air.

Both the combination dials and the outer doors had been removed. From where the dials had been, holes had been drilled into the spindles, one of which had reached its target. The second was jammed a quarter inch short of its correct depth. The guard realised immediately what had happened and raised the alarm.

Despite Banner's criminal record nobody thought to interview him about the raid, the bank just wanted to hush up the fact that someone had come close to breaching their security. There was no report in the *Times*, even the police were not encouraged to look very far: the Bank just wanted to hush it up.

They all held their breath for several weeks, but life went on as normal at the Bank. Stewart Banner sat down to plan another and better assault on the vault. He did not have long to wait, six months in fact.

Chapter 3 - The Team

Originally the Bank of America job was Freddie Leaf's idea: he had tried it with drills, but the drills didn't work. There was even talk of cutting through with a thermic lance, but he finally reckoned that the air conditioning would not be able to cope with the enormous amount of heat and fumes that would generate.

Before the first raid, both Stewart Banner and Freddie Leaf had been pretty active, with other little tickles just to keep the wolf from the door.

During that time Stewart had worked at a company called Duncan Watson also as an electrician. With a bit of help from his friends he had broken a factory window one evening, entered, and tried to blow the safe. One of his mates, an Irishman called Flaherty had provided the gelignite and detonators, but when it came to applying these to the safe, they made a right mess of its door, but it refused to open. They left empty handed.

Never one to quit, Stewart found another man who "knew a thing or two about blowing safes." By now however the room containing the safe was protected by a burglar alarm. Stewart and his new friend broke in and cut the wiring from the alarm. Just to see if the police had been alerted anyway, they retreated and watched the place from a safe distance. About twelve minutes later the boys in blue turned up, but did not notice Stewart and his friend driving away as casually as possible.

On another occasion, still keen to crack the mysteries of safe blowing, Stewart and some of his mates broke into the warehouse of Martins Newspapers Ltd near the Oval cricket ground. By sheer chance, whilst buying a newspaper, Stewart had seen one of the employees carrying some wage packets. He took a gander at the office where the man had come from, and spotted a safe.

He decided to involve a friend and have it away with the safe. Late that night they grabbed the safe and carried it away to a lockup. There they decided it was too risky to blow it, so they tried to lever the door open. After a few false starts, they finally 'peeled' the back off, a technique that only works with fairly old safes.

Far from containing money, it held vital office supplies: coffee, tea and sugar! But there was also a key in the safe. Not deterred they returned to the warehouse and found that the key fitted another safe. It opened, and there was the wages tin. This time they were £1,700 better off.

Freddie was keen to get into the antiques business. He could see that large amounts of money were made by not very clever, and rather limp wristed fellows, so he decided to cut himself a slice of that particular pie. Not even bothering to go very far from where he was staying, Freddie and Stewart applied their talents to a Kingston antiques shop. They prepared the job by replacing the lock on the premises with a barrel which would in fact take any Yale key, a trick which later came in handy at the Bank of America. Late one night they turned up with three tea chests and filled them with clocks to the tune of £4,500. Freddie sold them through his contacts to a fence, receiving perhaps 10% of their value. For his piece of work Banner received a mere £200.

Freddie and Stewart organised a more elaborate job at a rather posher antiques shop in the Kings Road, Chelsea. This time armed with a furniture van, they backed up to the shop after closing time, and simply loaded up various pieces of furniture, including antique writing desks, display cabinets, and a Queen Anne desk. This time the haul had a retail value of £17,000. They stored it in a lock up in Wimbledon, and when the heat had died down, fenced it in Bournemouth and via some of London's famous markets, where many a 'moody' piece gets sold before dawn. In these markets, anciently licensed as a 'market ouvert,' the real owner loses his title to the piece the moment it is sold to a new buyer, even if it is stolen.

For this work Freddie only gave Stewart £300.

They got a little tired of all the heavy lifting, and decided to do something a little more subtle. Freddie had broken into a film company just up the way from the Kings Road, in Pelham Street South Kensington, to have 'a look around,' when he stumbled on some cheque books. Very carefully he removed three cheques, not just the cheques, but also the counterfoils, with a razor blade, so that nobody using the cheque book in the normal way would notice that there was anything amiss. A little bit of not too complicated forgery, and Freddie paid the cheques into a newly opened bank account with Barclays, opened by Stewart. Freddie then drew £15,000 in cash and passed Stewart £550 for his help. Freddie figured that his living expenses were a bit higher than Stewart's.

Hearing from his brother, that a house in Chester Square had an interesting wall safe tucked away behind a picture, Freddie decided that Stewart should "go in and have a little look round." The idea was that Stewart would go along and pretend he was from the Post Office, which in those days was still responsible for the telephone system. When he got there he found that luck was on his side, and the maid had already let in some electricians to fit an alarm connected to the phone system.

When he rang the doorbell, in his Post Office overalls, the obliging maid said, "Are you with those two other men?" The gods were being good to him. He replied "Yes, love," and there he was in the house, free to wander round checking windows and doors, where ever he liked. He straight away went upstairs, into the bedroom, where he found a set of small keys which, with a bit of fiddling, opened the secret draws in the jewellery box. It was only a matter of seconds before the better pieces of 'tom' had found their way into Stewart's bogus Post Office tool box. He left without bothering to say goodbye.

The jewellery was worth £8,000, but after the fence had paid roughly 10% of this, and Freddie had taken his cut for the information, Stewart was left just with a few hundred in pin money.

His next job involved posing as a window cleaner, another tradesman about whom nobody gives a second thought. Stewart figured that a disguise and a bit of smooth talking was much easier than messing with jelly and dets, or heavy lifting. Freddie had discovered that there was a likely safe at the Chelsea Drug Store on the corner of the Kings Road and Royal Avenue, and had arranged to get a copy of the key that opened it. Stewart was to turn up with a team of real window cleaners, dressed the part, and stay behind when they left the premises. The idea was that he would stay the whole night, open the safe, and slip out next morning. However, someone told him there were rats on the premises, so not being fond of rats, he decided not to go through with the plan.

Finally Freddie got bored with London, or it got too hot for him, and he went away and got nicked for something he did abroad. So the Bank of America plan was sort of shelved for a while. Then the idea came up again — it was too good to leave alone, and the only way to do it properly would be to fully involve a good keyman, perhaps even the best keyman. So exactly six months after the first raid on the Bank of America they decided to do it again.

Another talented thief involved peripherally on the first raid was Jimmy O'Shaughnessy. He was light haired about five foot eight inches tall and quite good looking with intent blue eyes. Jimmy was born in 1943 to an Irish Catholic working class family, at the Putney end of the Kings Road, away from the glitter of the hippie revolution which took place there in the 1960s. He did however move into the burgeoning antiques trade by becoming an apprentice to a restorer of French antique furniture earning just eight pounds a week He also took up the trade of electrician, like Banner, as something that he could work at on a freelance basis.

He began to supplement these earnings with occasional forays into housebreaking, relying sometimes on information gathered in the course of his work. He went for posher targets than most of his early acquaintances. Jimmy always figured if the risks were roughly the same, always go for the bigger prize.

It was only a matter of time before he met with Freddie Leaf. Both men were interested in the antiques trade, particularly the sale of 'temporarily displaced' antiques of uncertain origin. Both found the Kings Road, with its ample supply of rich pickings, mini-skirted dolly birds, and late '60s laissez-faire to their liking. Both liked the good life, and each recognised the other as a cut above the rough and ready villains of the East End. Jimmy had no hesitation in using his fists, or anything else that came to hand if need be, but like Freddie he knew that the best prizes were those that could be finessed out of the clutches of their previous owners.

After doing a round of English country mansions, Jimmy expanded his operations to take in the French Riviera and the Spanish Costas especially Marbella, playground of the rich and famous. He was reputed to have been involved in a jewel theft from an Italian actress that made international headlines. Jimmy blended in with this set with his affable sense of humour, and he soon adopted the 'uniform' of mohair suits and cashmere jumpers.

After living in a flat in the West End for some time, he had bought in 1973 a largish five bedroom house set in its own grounds with its own gravely drive, in leafy Manorgate Road in the sedate suburb of Kingston-upon-Thames, in south west London. Over the period of a year or so he had done it up, virtually rebuilding the ground floor.

Just before the first raid on the Bank of America, he had finally moved into it with his girlfriend, Jane Spalding. At last he felt his life was falling into place, and that he had left the back streets of World's End behind. He had finally moved 'up the road," as he used to refer to the inhabitants of the Kings Road proper or indeed the middle class gentility of Kingston. Jimmy was 32 and thought that it was time he and his girlfriend Jane Spalding settled down. They had been together for quite a while, and were for all intents and purposes a married couple. Meanwhile Jane had landed a good job as the private secretary to the Ambassador of one of the Scandinavian countries.

Freddie Leaf, by now an old friend, had been invited to actually stay with Jimmy in his house at Manorgate Road, when the idea of doing the Bank of America first came up.

When Freddie Leaf put Stewart Banner up to the first Bank of America robbery in October 1974, he looked round for some likely lads to put together a team. After discussing it with Jimmy, he had asked Willy Gavroche, who was a well-known villain and bookie, or turf accountant as he preferred to be known. Willy lived fairly comfortably in Bishop's Park Road, in Streatham, SW16, in south west London. Willy was tall and quite striking with tattoos and a mop of ginger hair. He was easy to spot in a crowd, and a pretty smart operator. They both liked the idea of having him along on the job: he was a born comic.

When I say villain, I don't mean he was a particularly nasty person, quite the contrary, I just mean he was professional thief. There are probably people who you know well, and yet you may not know that they are actually thieves, ranging from the occasional opportunist to the habitual professional. Thieves occur in all walks of life. They can be amongst the most charming people. Willy Gavroche is a gentleman, and he was amongst the first to be asked by Leaf to help do the first job.

What Freddie and Jimmy wanted to do was to get a little team of people together because they knew it wasn't going to be a two minute job. You had to be in there for a long time, opening the safety deposit boxes, it might even be an overnight thing. There would be a lot of heavy 'caning' and carrying. They also needed a couple of reliable lookouts.

When Freddie gave up on the first raid, Jimmy became the brains and main mover behind the second raid. Freddie, if you like, gave the job to Jimmy. Jimmy couldn't get over how close they had been to breaking the Bank the first time around.

It was Jimmy really who did the detailed planning for the second attempt. Willy is game for anything, but Jimmy like Freddie is a thinker. So they got it into their heads, a couple of months later, to do it again, but this time they thought, we'll have a keyman, a lock expert to help with the vault itself, who can do more than just provide keys for the back door.

Anyway Jimmy decided not to waste what they knew, and to go in again, with the same firm plus a few more game people. Jimmy did not want to do it as a robbery, going in and holding everybody up at gunpoint, so he had to get someone to cut the keys, so they went again to Johnny Wilde.

I don't know if it was Willy Gavroche or Jimmy O'Shaughnessy, but I've got a feeling it was Willy, who first approached Johnny and said "we want to do the Bank of America again." Willy offered Johnny a deal and said to him, "if you cut the keys, we'll give you £20,000 pounds", because that was Johnny's speciality job. That wasn't a bad fee in 1974, for a couple of day's work.

"He's such a pro, Johnny," he said "Yeah? It's nothing to do with me. I don't hold up anyone."

They said, "no we don't want to rob it, run in with guns and stick it up, we want to burgle it. But we need someone to cut the keys."

They were clever really, because there were only two people clever enough to cut those keys, and he was one. The other one was a Scots keyman. Key cutting is sometimes a matter of trial and error. It was very seldom with Johnny that you had to go back and amend the keys time & time again. Whereas the other fella, who is retired now, often had to cut and then cut again. For him you had to blacken the key blanks or the first cut key with a match. Say for example if you had a Yale, you had to burn it with a lighter so that it all went black, then put it in the lock and turn the key. If it didn't open, the soot from the flame would be marked by the obstinate tumblers. You could then take it back to the keyman and he'd cut them out again. They couldn't really afford too much of that kind of nonsense, so they went to Johnny.

Johnny thought for only a few seconds about the offer, before he turned round and said "I'll tell you what I'll do, I'll cut the keys providing I'm on it. I want a piece of the action."

It didn't take Johnny more than a few seconds to figure that a sixth or even a tenth of a million pounds minimum was somewhat better than £20,000, and once he had cut the keys, his signature was as good as all over the job anyway, so he said "I'm in, but on an equal share with the rest of you."

When Johnny said "I want my share of it, not just £20,000 for a couple of keys, or whatever" he didn't know that they were to come out of there with £8 million in cash and up to £26 million total including the gold and jewellery. From a purely financial point of view he definitely made the right decision.

So Johnny was on the job, and the meetings began. They had to recruit different people with other special skills. Johnny invited Paul Caldwell, a part-time car dealer, from the same part of London as himself, and who drank in the same pub to join the 'firm.' Paul Caldwell was 32 and fair haired. He had a great love of fast cars, good living, eating in the right restaurants, and being seen with the right people. He even had one of the first swimming pools in his part of London: in the end though, the police dug up his swimming pool. That pissed him off no end. I can't think whether they really thought the loot was buried under it, or if the excavation was just motivated by sheer envy.

He always had at least three cars to hand. One was a lovely blue Mercedes, another was a very expensive Lamborghini. He certainly like to flaunt it, when he had it. His third car was an E-type Jaguar. I had an E-type in 1969: lovely cars they were, they cost then about £2,000 and were 'the' status symbol of those years. You can still go and buy them, but they cost a lot more now, and you daren't drive them about London, with those nonexistent bumper bars and the high cost of special insurance. Even in the late sixties parking them without scratching them was a bit of a problem!

Another real pro, Mickey Jevons, who had been on the first raid, was invited to join the second attempt. He was only eventually charged with conspiracy in the first raid. He was 32 at the time, and an electrician just like Banner and Jimmy. Between these three there was nothing they couldn't do when it came to electricity.

Afterwards Mickey was to go on to do some pretty daring robberies, like the great Silver Bullion robbery, but we will come to those later. By the age of 37 he had stolen millions from bank vaults and jewelers, and in all that time he only did the one 18-month sentence. The proceeds of these raids was spent on high living across Europe. He was quite tall and rather lanky if I remember right, and slightly balding but with very intelligent eyes. Some of his friends used to call him 'Skinny.' He was in many ways another very very smart man.

It's funny because I don't usually take notice of those sort of things, but I remember him as being a very smart person. He was quite a playboy, he liked the ladies, particularly the dark eyed ones. I knew he used to travel quite a lot, and his passport was stuffed with stamps. In fact when he was in the money, he thought nothing of popping over to Paris just for afternoon tea. Detective Chief Inspector Bill Peters of the Robbery Squad described him as "a very, very intelligent man, probably the most intelligent criminal I ever met."

At that point, there were six main people on the job, but there were also a lot of 'soldiers' apart from them, who were involved in it, for a 'drink' or fixed fee, for procuring cars or equipment or giving specialised advice on alarms or whatever.

Freddie Maiser's son was then suggested as someone who would be useful if there was a ruck, and because of his father's influence in the 'business.' Freddie Maiser junior was about 20 and rough, rough, rough. Not fat, not a very big person, I think he had brown hair, but he was very tough. In many ways it was odd for Freddie to be in on the job, everyone else came from either north-west or south-west London. Freddie was from Elephant and Castle, a whole different ball game. And in that part of London they used to play hard ball.

Chapter 4 - Johnny Wilde

Let me first tell you a few things more about Johnny Wilde. He was 51 at the time, and had mousey coloured hair. He was about five nine, wasn't stocky, wasn't thin either. His hair's gone completely grey by now, but as I say I haven't seen him for several years. Johnny didn't have tattoos like some of the others. He was quiet, and kept himself to himself.

He's a funny character, in his way. He's dry, serious miserable fucker. He must be an old man now, but I always found it hard to think of Johnny as an old man.

His real name was something else altogether, but early on he adopted a name from the name of the area where he lived. He always seemed fairly well off, and had invested in several greengrocer's shops. He lived with his very much younger wife Vivienne in Palmers Green, London N13. He also had another more discreet property just round the corner in Hedge Lane.

Vivienne was into anything, and had always had boyfriends from amongst the 'fraternity.' Some of the team thought that Johnny should just do the keys and sit back, and that he was too old for this kind of caper, but Johnny could see the potential and demanded to come along.

They reckon Johnny was the best keyman in England if not in the world. Old Bill, themselves, reckon there is not a man to touch him for making a key. Johnny was known as 'the Bosh," because he invented a tool that would open a car, any car, and turn on the ignition, just like that.

We used to say "Johnny, we want to nick that motor, all right then," and he would go and get the tool. He wouldn't let anybody else have it, he would just walk out to the car and do it. He used to say, "look I'll bosh it over for you, and sort out the whole central locking system." He used to put this thing in it and bosh it off, couldn't have been simpler. That's why they called him the Bosh.

Johnny had had a reputation for being the best for a long time. He had been asked to do the keys for Ronnie Biggs's attempted escape from the Maximum Security Wing of HMP Aylesbury, and he had obliged back in 1965. Even then Ronnie Biggs referred to him as "a legendary key maker known as Johnny the Bosh." On this job Johnny worked from knowledge of the brand of lock and a sketch made by another of the Great Train Robbers, of the key hanging from the belt of one of the screws who was playing chess with Ronnie Biggs at the time. That is all he needed to know to make a key that worked perfectly. As it happened this particular escape plan was thwarted when Bill Shoal spilled the beans to the prison governor.

I'll tell you what he's like. Once in the late 1960s we went into a builder's merchants down Fulham way, to get some materials. I always used to look at the safes, so I said "I bet you can't do that one." They had a new safe in this builder's merchants down in Fulham. I went "I bet you can't do that one."

He went "that's the new Thompson's" whatever. He said "Yes" he could do it, "it's only a tin can." But the geezer behind the counter heard him. He said "You couldn't do that thing mate!"

If you look at Johnny, you wouldn't think he was anything special. Very softly he says "I think if I wanted to, I suppose I could." The bloke said "Nah, they couldn't. You couldn't. I'm telling you mate, I know when I buy gear it's the right stuff." I said "Oh all right, don't get nasty about it. Can I have me timber and bits of plasterboard and I'll go."

I dragged Johnny out of there, put them in my motor and was gone. That night he went in there, made a key for the door, opened the safe with a key he made, took the money out of the safe and put it in the right hand drawer of the desk. He left a note in the safe with some dog shit, saying "look in the right drawer of your desk shit face, and see about your peter (safe) that can't be done!" He never took the money, which was the sort of person he was. He did things which might have put him right on the line, just to teach some stupid prick a lesson. They didn't know who he was. He didn't come from Fulham, did he? We never went in there again.

Another time, he got done and the police fitted him up with explosives. He got 10 years for it. When he came out he really had the hump about it, because he hadn't done it, and they actually did fit him up. What he did was, a little revenge on the copper that nicked him and the judge that sent him down. He virtually proved, in court, that it wasn't what they said, but because of their determination, because they were corrupt, and because they could do what they liked in court, they gave him 10 years.

He first took his revenge on the judge. He made the key for his house, the key to turn his alarm off and gave the bit of work to someone else and said, "Rob him, take everything you can and keep it. I don't want anything." And then he did the copper. He didn't do this every day, but he went and took his car from the police pound and put it outside the door of the copper's house, when he was at work. Must have freaked him a bit. And then another time he took it from outside his house and put it in the police pound, behind the police station. He did that 5 or 6 times, it was driving the copper mad. That's why they called him the 'Bosh,' because he could bosh any lock on any door on any car, and drive it away as fast as the owner with a key.

Him and his wife Viv were funny, she was a lot younger than him by 18 years, but because he had plenty of money, he had bundles of money, she fell for him. When they used to row, because he'd been inside so much, he used to go and lock himself in the top bedroom. He wouldn't come out for three days. You'd think he was on bread and water, or something. He would starve himself deliberately. He didn't care.

He knew she was carrying on with other blokes. So one time he got a tin of silver paint and made a slight hole in it and tied it to her car, you won't believe this. He taped it to her car, 10 minutes before she was going out and he followed the car using the line of silver paint spatters! He hated that, but knew it was the price he paid for having an attractive much younger bird.

He was a very private person, and a bit older than the other blokes. Willy Gavroche said to Johnny one day "can I borrow your car on Sunday?" Johnny said at first "no," but Willy needed it very desperately. He finally relented and said, "OK, but don't do anything iffy in it." Willy said he was just going to visit a 'cousin.'

Johnny's car was a Triumph Dolomite Sprint with a souped up motor. Willy borrowed the car, but when he was using it he happened to throw his empty cigarette packet out of the car window. The bloke behind, a prize prick, him took the number of the car.

A week or so later Johnny got an official letter. He didn't know what it was about, it just said he had to report to the court or give an admission of guilt, and be fined in his absence. He worked out the dates and figured it was when Willy had the car — he was very astute, Johnny — he didn't know what it was about so he fills the form in 'Not Guilty.' He sends it back in, and they send him another letter stating that he has to be in court on a certain date.

So he goes to court, finds out that he's nicked, finds out what it's for, gets his name and address taken, then Johnny says, "I'll plead guilty to that" pays his £20 fine and goes home. But he has got the hump. He demands to know who witnessed, the 'offence," and he writes it down.

Then he starts. Every newspaper he got, anything that was going or advertised, he'd send it to the address of the bloke who complained. It cost him money — he had wreaths sent to him, flowers sent to him, dildoes sent to him, dirty books sent to him, kitchen suites sent to him, he done him up like a kipper, for months. Then one day, this bloke got tired and reported him, every bleeding incident.

The affair even got on to local television. The interviewer asks him "who do you think is causing this vendetta against you?"

It got a bit out of order it did, so Johnny made a key for his house, went in there and turned all his furniture round. Didn't do anything else. He put the couch from over there to here. He put the telly from here to there — he moved everything around. He did the same to his bedroom. You can imagine what he thought when he got home. So the fella rings up the police and reports it again.

Then one night he went up to the bloke's house, about one o'clock in the morning, with a hungry nanny goat — this is true — opened the bloke's door and tied the nanny goat to the newel post at the bottom of the stairs and left, and went home. The nanny made a right mess of his hall.

A few months later he did it again.

Every time he did it he kept leaving him a message, a clue, because Johnny was like that — he used to do crosswords all day long — and liked other people to use their brains occasionally as well. Then he decided that that was it, he reckoned he was going to do the last thing, and then that was it. He knew the bloke went to work every day religiously at eight o'clock. He's already made a key for his house door, so he's gone in to the bloke's house, took off his shirt — he's got a vest on — got shaving soap and put it round his face. He looks right at home.

There's a knock on the door, it's the delivery man with the manure. He's ordered the manure. He says, "Here mate, here's the twenty pound, back it over that fence, knock it down, over the hedge, and put it outside the window." The bloke says "are you sure?" He's says "here's twenty pounds," so the driver does it. He's driven off.

About half hour later the cement lorry came round. He does the same thing to the bloke. Here's twenty pounds. He's got this towel over his shoulder, half shaving, he really looks like an authentic resident. "Back it over there, mate, on top of that." The bloke looked at him but he gave him the money, then Johnny just washed himself and left. That was his last calling card. On the news they asked the man "whose doing this vendetta?" He said "well let's put it this way, I will never interfere again."

That's the sort of person Johnny was. He was a bit of a loner. Although he's quite well known to the fraternity, he's not that well known outside. The police know him better than anybody else.

There was a copper told me that even the screws used his services. Once Johnny was banged up waiting below a court to go up for trial. While he was sitting in the cells someone's run off with the key to the sugar and tea cupboard, for the screws. They can't get in to their tea cupboard. So they knock Johnny up and say "can you have a look at this for us?" He says "yeah, I don't see why not. Have you got a pen on you?" And he used the end of the pen. He wouldn't let them see him do it. He used the end of the pen and bent it back. He said "here you are." The door just popped open.

Whenever I went to see him indoors he was always playing with locks. Sitting down with four or five types of locks, working out the levers. He took it all very seriously, he even used to send to France for special metal to make keys with. When he talked about locks he always talked about single levers, double levers, and double this or that. He'd almost get an orgasm taking them to pieces and putting them back together again, and working out the leverage. He was that sort of a person. He used to tell me "I love it when I get there and there are five or six really good locks on. If they put silly little locks on, I get frustrated with them for putting the fucking little things on. They might as well not bother, but when they put the good ones there and I've got to graft and work it, I really love it." He used to get a buzz out of his work. It's a real skill to be able to do a thing like that. He was quite a character.

He walked into a shop one day, with his missus, to buy some furniture at about quarter past five on a Saturday, the shop shuts at half past and the geezer wants to go home. Johnny wants to buy some furniture, so he picks out a three piece suite, a Chesterfield. He picks out a sideboard and he picks out a couple of chairs. The bill comes to three thousand and seventy four pounds. Johnny says "I'll give you three grand cash, now." Nowadays they'd bite your hand off for a cash deal like that. Still even in those days they could have done.

He was a cocky little berk the salesman, and he didn't believe Johnny had the money. He said "have you got the money? I've got to have three thousand and seventy four pounds."

Johnny says "No, I'll give you three grand cash now." The bloke went "no chance, mate."

Johnny said, "look I'm gonna give you your last chance." The bloke had a go at him. He said "Who do you think you are talking to me like that. I run this shop, and we don't do things like that."

Johnny said "Well please yourself mate, I offered you a deal." So he left.

Later that Saturday night he made a key for the shop, and made a key to open and start their vans — they had two big furniture vans at the back. He walked down the High Street, talked to a couple of lively chaps and said "do you want a bit of work? All you've got to do is go down there and load up. You've got all tonight and tomorrow to do it. I guarantee there's no bells."

They said "Yeah, we'll have some of that, Johnny." He said, "there is one condition, you must leave the Chesterfield, the sideboard, and the two chairs right in the middle of the shop. But I want the whole shop cleared, right down to the junk. Here's the keys."

They did it. They cleared the whole shop out on the Sunday morning. When the bloke walked in on Monday morning he saw an empty shop except for the sideboard, the Chesterfield and two chairs. Johnny just hated bullshit. It was not till much later that putting a cheeky salesman in his place was to cost Johnny a whole lot more than he had bargained for.

Another time, we went to a restaurant, me, him and two birds we were trying to impress, went into an Italian restaurant in Pimlico, near Victoria. What do I know about Italian food? What does

Johnny know about Italian food?

We're trying to be Charlie Bananas with the two birds. Actually, I was the one trying to be Charlie Bananas with two birds.

I was doing most of the chat, because Johnny's a bit older than me. We ordered a meal. We didn't know what we were ordering. Johnny didn't know, and the birds didn't know. The waiters obviously knew. We had this horrible meal, it was like eating kippers and custard.

I said "I want to punch the geezer's lights out I gotta tell you. He knew we didn't know and just wanted to make fun of us. That Italian — I really want to hurt him because he's mugged us right off." But Johnny laughed it off.

Johnny went "excuse me, could I see the manager please?" The manager came and Johnny said "Look, take that away — I've paid for it. Just take it away." He said, "but I'd like you to tell your waiter that that was out of order, what he's done." He said "he knew we was ordering wrong. Why did he let us go through with the order?"

The bloke said "well you ordered it, you get what you order, OK?" Johnny looked me in the face and said "Oh, all right then." Johnny looked carefully round the place then he says "I'm just going to the toilet." As he was going to the toilet there was a coat rack nearby, and the keys to the safe and the shop all hung up. I saw his hand go to them. Later he's at home in his shed, and he's cutting the keys. He returned to the restaurant, and I think he took ten and a half grand.

Just out of pure annoyance — he didn't need ten and a half grand. And he left them a note saying "next time you sell punters a meal put them on the right track." It could have been anybody. If they'd have come and checked the keys they'd have found none of them missing anyway, if the police had been involved. They wouldn't have even thought it was Johnny.

Johnny however did have a reputation with the police. If anything really clever happens with keys in London, where keys are concerned they'll go to see Johnny. Similarly, if anything with high explosives is involved they go to Jerry Mancini, because of his ability with explosives. That is how the police work. They use their knowledge of specialities.

Chapter 5 - Planning the Job

Freddie Leaf by now had left for sunnier climes. The core team was by then Stewart Banner as inside man, Johnny Wilde as keyman, Jimmy O'Shaughnessy as the architect, Paul Caldwell, Willy Gavroche, and Mickey Jevons as practiced thieves, and Freddie Maiser junior as muscle and backup.

They were a great team if you knew them, Willy Gavroche was a natural comic, an out and out comedian, and so was Paul in his own way, while the most serious person out of all them was Johnny. They planned and they re-planned. They were all strong personalities, and each had his own answer to the various problems. They had so many rucks about the planning of this job, I tell you. They had about ten, twelve planning meetings. They had rucks on eight of them.

Nobody really knew how big the job was going to be. Nobody expected to get what they got out of it, but they knew that they had to have more bodies in there for the safety deposit boxes, because they had to open as many as possible of them in a short time. They also needed good lookouts who would keep their bottle and not just fade away if Old Bill turned up mob handed.

Planning meetings were held first in a pub, and then later on Wimbledon Common so that they couldn't be overheard. Originally it had been just friends and close contacts. In the end we had a mixed team, a couple of people from North London (Mickey Jevons, Paul Caldwell, Johnny Wilde), a couple of people from South London (Jimmy O'Shaughnessy, Stewart Banner, and Willy Gavroche), Freddie Maiser from down the Old Kent Road, and a couple on the fringes from the East End.

Anyway, Jimmy, who was doing most of the sorting out, arranged one of these meetings on Wimbledon Common. They all nearly fell out at this meeting. Why the flipping hell they want to meet on the Common, I don't know. It did look a bit strange all these people walking about on the Common, deep in argument in the middle of the day. They nearly fell out because, contrary to what people think, North London people and East London don't get on with South London people.

The same with East Enders who don't get on with South Londoners. There is always that friction, that little bit of distrust, between them. Perhaps it dates back to the Kray's friction with the Richardson's south London gang. Mainly I guess it's the way they talk. East Enders don't really mean what they say, but they're more 'the business.'

For example if you went in to rob a bank, an East Ender, nine times out of ten, would "put one in the lid," fire a barrel at the ceiling, just to make sure everyone's paying attention. The customers are then really frightened of the gun and know he means business. A North Londoner is likely to go in there and shout "everybody on the floor" and begin shouting and growling. The East Ender, he'll go that one bit further and put one in the lid so that with the bang, the noise, the falling plaster and the shouting, the customers and staff definitely get on the floor and won't bother to ponce about.

Because of these differing temperaments there were quite a few rows before the actual robbery was committed. There was nearly a punch-up between Freddie Maiser, who is a bit mouthy anyway at the best of times and Paul Caldwell who resented his presence, "What are you doing here in on this for anyway Freddie, eh?"

"Listen, Caldwell, you want your teeth down your throat then just keep on like that." After all Freddie was there because his dad had a lot of pull, not because he was close friends with any of them. There was that element in any group when people don't click, but we also had to respect the fact that each person was guaranteed by the person who introduced them, that they were kosher and they were all right. Who introduced who is an important element when the chips are down and

The Mayfair Bank Job

the possibility of one member grassing the other rears its ugly head.

Freddie Maiser for example was in because of his father, but he never got nicked for the Bank of America robbery, they knew he did it, the police, but he never got nicked. Such was the extent of his family's 'influence.' Freddie knew O'Shaughnessy, and Jimmy wanted a bit of help with a few of the technical details, and Freddie's father knew just where to put his hand on them.

In the end Freddie got a diamond out of the job as big as a hen's egg. I'll tell you afterwards where that went. He cut it into 42 diamonds, which the police found. They had to give it back to him, because they had no proof. He said he bought the 42 diamonds in Amsterdam and they couldn't prove otherwise.

To safeguard their inside man, Banner wasn't actually there on the job itself. There were also two or three others from the East End to help with the boxes and act as lookouts on both sets of stairs, in Davies Street, and in the Yard behind the Bank, that I didn't know. They were all from different parts of London, and each only knew certain other people.

You can imagine in a case like this someone painstakingly sticking something together, a piece of work, gradually assembling the necessary skills by involving the right people, but being careful to restrict essential knowledge on a need to know basis. The less people knew the less they could grass. Only two of them knew the night they were going to strike, only myself and four others knew where the slaughter was, and only six or seven knew which bank we were going to hit. In all about 15 people knew something was 'on.'

The same principles involved in putting the 'firm' together applied to the Great Train Robbery, the previous biggest robbery before the Bank of America. Someone for example comes up to you and says "we're going to do a robbery." Now he knows he's in a room full of game people, and somebody is going to say "I'll have a piece of that." Then before that person is on the job, a lot of talking has to be done.

The Mayfair Bank Job

Sticking together a piece of work also involves checking with other firms who might have similar plans. You don't want to fall over each other on the night. That is how the big boys like Freddie Maiser's father get to hear about jobs being done on their patch. When the Great Train Robbers told me not to go ahead with that bit of work at London Airport because they had something big on, they were bigger league people than me. I realised that I wasn't in their league, so I backed off. Maybe I regret missing that opportunity, but the likes of Gordon Goody and Roy James were that little bit older than me, at the time, and I sort of respected them.

When in 1963 the Train Robbers said "do you fancy coming on this bit of work with us, it's worth about £1 million," well your first reaction has got to have been "it's not possible is it?" It's like if someone said to you today, "would you like to come in on the bit of work we have got on, which is going to be worth £26 million." You'd think he was dreaming, wouldn't you? Well you would do, wouldn't you? You wouldn't actually believe that there is that much money around, certainly not in one bank vault.

When Freddie Leaf started setting up the first Bank of America raid, someone had already done the safety deposit vaults at Lloyds Bank in Baker Street, so there was a precedent. I think it was one of the first large safety deposits vaults to go. Later this sort of thing became popular in France.

Everyone, including Freddie, were speculating about how much they got from Lloyds, but nobody was talking. So we were guessing. I didn't know everybody who did it, actually I only know one bloke who was on it, but he's got nothing now, and he wasn't about to talk about it then. It does not matter what the papers say about how much they got, with a job like a safety deposit vault, where the contents are not recorded even by the bank, only the robbers actually know how much they took, and even then the jewellery is difficult to value.

The largest safe deposit job subsequently done in the UK was the Knightsbridge Safety Deposit Vault job in 1987, but even though they caught some of the firm, nobody knows quite how much money actually was stolen, although estimates pitch it around £30-40 million. It was all in private boxes. The firm that did it was stuck together by an Italian, who if he had not left one tiny blood filled finger print, and if he had not insisted upon continually returning to the UK to buy yet another Ferrari, might well have got away with it.

We sat there and speculated. The Bank of America might have £1 million, or maybe more. Without a knowledge of the contents of other safety deposit vaults it was impossible to judge. The bank looked like a small office premises from the outside, but its combination of American offshore status, closeness to Claridge's and the American Embassy in the heart of Mayfair, made it a much bigger catch than even Freddie Leaf had guessed in his wildest dreams, and Freddie had some pretty wild dreams.

Freddie and Jimmy knew from the abortive first attempt in 1974 what the setup was, so when Jimmy said to us, "well I've got the ability, we can get in and do it," then you could half believe it. You've got to be pretty into a job before committing yourself, and you have got to see that the other people on the firm can really do their bit. Then it's not a dream world any more, all of a sudden it's a reality that could happened. We always thought that they had millions out of the Lloyds Bank, but apparently they didn't have as much as we thought. But whatever they got, even if we were only going to get £½ million, then it's not a bad night's work, you know what I mean.

I didn't know how big it was when I was brought into it by Johnny, nor did I know everybody who was in on the job. I know they had regular meetings, and during the preparation period they used to talk to each other a lot. We used to say, "it will be nice if it comes off," you know what I mean, and all this old nonsense, half believing our own propaganda, half doubting that we could bring off such a big one.

We speculated, "Why aren't they better protected" and "Maybe there is something we still don't know." Maybe it was because the Bank was more discreet than most, that they felt they wouldn't be targeted. Even after the first hit they were pretty cool about their security. They had the vaults built specially in the basement. They were sure nobody could tunnel into it because the vault itself was like an island in the basement, totally surrounded by corridors. Anyone tunneling in would have to finish up in that corridor, before starting to cut through the six to eight foot thick walls of the vault itself. As the corridor was supposed to be regularly checked by a security man, I guess they felt pretty confident.

Taking into account all the preparation for the first attempt the second attempt was about a year in preparation, quite a long time really. They did the preparation really well, with Banner on the inside to tell them about any electrical modifications to the alarm system. Amazingly, Banner was actually responsible for the wiring of the Bank's new alarm system. They knew that they could get to the actual doors of the vaults, they knew that Johnny had broken the drills trying to do it before, and so they could make a reasonable amount of noise, and they knew the team had got away without interruption or being spotted. Banner hadn't even had a pull from the police after the first raid, so why should he worry about the second one. They knew that it could be done.

Nowadays such an opportunity is like a dream, because now payrolls are paid into banks and bank accounts all by direct credits. No large quantities of money are kept as cash, and no information comes out about it if it is. Local bank branches, even with good strong-rooms, tend to keep the minimum amount of cash. They would sooner run out of cash than be vulnerable. Now, and then, the most detailed information that comes out about any potential for bank robberies comes from the police themselves. Police actually sometimes stuck up jobs, I know you are going to find it hard to believe, but for a consideration of sometimes only £5000, they put such jobs as armoured car and bank robberies on offer to select members of the fraternity.

The Mayfair Bank Job

Police were the only people that knew the exact movement of large quantities of money, because they're guarding it. As part of this protection, they had to put out special patrols, so they're not obviously sitting behind it in case someone hits it. Ordinary police in local nicks become aware of this extra activity, and can easily figure out what is going on. So they're amongst the first people to know, unless there is an actual inside man, so they can stick up this kind of work.

With the Bank of America, there was no such police involvement, but it had to be an inside job. So when Banner came out of jail and applied for a job in there and got it, the first plan came together rapidly. Leaf was lucky in finding his old accomplice in such a key position, and didn't take him long to take advantage of this.

The second attempt was really Jimmy O'Shaughnessy's dream, he saw how the first attempt almost succeeded and couldn't wait to make the attempt again, but this time with better preparation. Meanwhile the Bank had not really strengthened its defenses.

Johnny Wilde had been involved with the first drilling attempt, and he was even more necessary to the second attempt. So it was not a big deal when he said to me, "Oi, do you want to work the slaughter, drive me up to Mayfair with my gear, and then go on to the slaughter?"

He said to me, "do you want ten grand, to be at the slaughter, and you can get rid of the shit." Ten grand wasn't bad for a night's work in the mid-seventies. I was in. Johnny had always been very cool even casual about his work.

If I'd had a special talent that would have been needed to be part of it, then I would have got more. Although, I've never understood what Freddie Maiser's talent was, except for being well connected. Mickey Jevons had special talents, he had the gift of the gab, like a con man, and he looked respectable so he could talk his way into and out of, all sorts of situations. He also had a lot of bottle. When they did the Silver Bullion job later in 1980 they stopped a truck, and he pretended to be policemen. Cool as a cucumber he imitated a cozzer. He was good at keeping his bottle. He was well connected, he was in with everybody.

Jimmy was the dream boy that got the idea off Leaf. He had to take it to someone: he couldn't cope with that on his own. He needed people who could do things, and Mickey Jevons was definitely a good addition to the team.

Willy Gavroche has always been a thief in his own way, be it a warehouse, a post office hold up or whatever. Paul Caldwell has been the same, and comes from a family who were all part of the fraternity.

You see, because I've always worked I've always been on the fringe. Because I'm not there all the time. I didn't see the percentage in being there all the time because they were always 'going away' for two or three years and then coming out. It didn't really appeal to me. So I always went to work. It's not just a case of being brainy, or if you go to work you're not getting nicked so much. It's in my system that I've always worked. I'm one of these people that's always worked.

If I won the pools tomorrow I'd still work. I just wouldn't get up so bleeding early in the morning. I wasn't really that 'active.' They would be at it all day, in the boozer drinking and doing nothing else for months. Then they'd have it off. I wasn't prepared to take that chance that you might have it off. So I was quite happy, being a small time crook, getting little bits and pieces here and there but still working, getting her indoors money. So that's why, the only reason some of them were in on it, was because they were the 'in' crowd.

On April 3, 1975 two of the Great Train Robbers were let out after finishing their sentences. That is just 21 days before the second Bank of America robbery came off. It is fascinating to speculate about the possible connection between these two enormous robberies. Maybe it was just coincidence. One was Buster Edwards, the other was Jimmy White.

The Mayfair Bank Job

Other Great Train Robbers came out soon after. Gordon Goody came out of prison a few days before Christmas 1975: he had got £150,000 and done twelve years for it. Anyway it was certainly a cause for celebration, and it gave everybody's spirits a lift.

I was there the night he came out at the drink up, down at the Duke's Head in Putney, on Lower Richmond Road. Because he asked me to chat a bird up for him. Yeah, she kept looking at him. She had a mini skirt on. He hadn't even seen a mini skirt: he had missed out on the Carnaby street thing.

I said "go on and give it a pull." He said "I can't. Go over and talk to her for me." I just walked over to the bird. I said "Do you know who that is?" She said "no."

I said "that's Checker, Gordon Goody, one of the Great Train Robbers." I said, "he's got a nice few quid." She said "Oh yeah, I'll join the company." And so she did: everyone was happy.

Johnny was the same generation as the Great Train Robbers and knew them. It seems that most of these guys have been involved in one way or another in lots of the big robberies. It is just a small group of people that are involved in big robberies. It seems to be the same top twenty catchers in the country were involved in most of the big things.

If a big robbery normally went off, it didn't take that long for the police to draw up a list of twenty or so 'possibles,' and start checking their alibis. There wasn't that much amateur talent doing the big jobs. So if a person came from outside the country, say a French man and did a bank job in England they wouldn't know who the hell did it. Indeed they only caught the Italian who did the Knightsbridge job because he kept coming back, not just to London, but also to the very same hotel.

Sometimes English criminals go and do a job in Europe, like Freddie, and that makes them much harder to spot, except they do stick out a bit in the boozers. He used to do the old till trick. And eventually he got nicked and did a bit of bird over there. He was quite an active, clever person he was, quite a clever burglar.

I know for a fact that Johnny went a couple of times, he was in Spain and he did whatever he did out there. His main problem was that he had done it while he was on holiday. He used the holiday as a cover with people and slipped off and did what he had to do. He was so good he could literally make the keys and just slip in and out of a place. He used to have to go and bury the stuff, and then go back at a later date and pick it up because, obviously, airports and shipping ports were all being watched quite thoroughly, after such a job, for known faces such as him. Anyway for the job in hand, everyone was a local lad, which made it that much easier for the cozzers.

Anyway, the planning proceeded, and gradually a new plan was being stuck together. They still could not agree on how they were actually going to get through the actual vault door itself, until a blinding stroke of good luck intervened...

Chapter 6 - Spying the Combination

There was nobody in the basement of the Bank of America's premises at Davies Street Mayfair in early spring of 1975 to appreciate the full irony of the electrical repair job being undertaken by Stewart Banner. He had been briefed to help install a new alarm system, which had been insisted upon by the bank's management following the October 1974 attempt to rob the bank's vault. That the raid had been a failure, was a fact well known to Banner, as he had helped to plan it.

Luckily for him, no one had suspected his involvement in spite of his criminal record. He had not even been questioned. The Bank had been more concerned to hush things up as fast as possible. The holes in their vault doors could be filled, welded and hidden. The new steel plugs were in fact stronger than the door they were set into. The Bank's customers need never know how close they had come to losing the contents of their safety deposit boxes.

After all, the management reasoned, lightning never strikes twice in the same place. The vault doors had successfully stopped the thieves, they would not be back for a second try. If anything, the bank's management were confirmed in their view of the impregnability of their defenses, but a new alarm would not go amiss to reassure head office in America, that their London branch was in good hands.

The thieves were not in fact put off by their first failure, but even more determined to go after the glittering prizes locked up behind the vault doors which Banner was in the process of 'protecting' with a new alarm. Banner, not driven to making grand plans as was Freddie Leaf, was nevertheless fascinated by the challenge of bypassing the bank's defenses.

While searching for a way to lead a power line to within reach of the bank's huge vault doors, so that any future attempt at drilling through would be well supplied with power, Banner climbed inside a suspended ceiling just above the vault door. The anteroom to the vault was quite small, about eight feet by five. The problem was to bypass the main electrical feed to the switchboard and the new security system, so these could be put out of action while still having a power supply for the drill.

He was running out of time, there were only 20 minutes to go before the bank closed for the day, and he began to get clumsy in an effort to finish in time. He attempted to fix a connector block to a loose live wire, something he would not normally do, but there was no time to go and switch off the power first. He fumbled the wire and it sprang out of his hands near to his face. He jumped back rapidly, and in his haste he drove his screw driver through one of the false ceiling tiles.

Swearing under his breath and being careful to avoid the still live wire, lying there like a snake ready to sting him with all of its venomous 240 volts, he peered through the hole he had made. Suddenly he heard voices. "Damn," he thought, "that's all I need," as he recognised the American twang of Steve the manager and his chief cashier Dave who were approaching the front of the vault door. They opened the door and stepped into the anteroom.

He froze, not wishing to draw attention to his recent piece of destruction, or the fact that he was not strictly where he should have been. He didn't really mind that, but explaining it to the picky chief cashier was not exactly what he had in mind for this evening.

He peered down through the hole he had made. Banner was amazed to find himself almost directly above the other two, and that through the hole in the ceiling tile he could clearly see the vault door itself. The door had two separate combination locks set into its front. Security relied upon each combination number only being known to one man, so that both were necessary to open the door. Neither man knew the other's number, a precaution which was backed up by vertical steel shields which made it impossible for either man to watch the dial turns of the other. The shields however did not pass over the top of the dials, and Banner, lying quietly 3 feet above the two bank officers was amazed to find himself with a grandstand view of one of the dials.

Each dial had to be turned four times alternatively to the left and then the right till an exact number marked on the top of the dial came into view. Overshooting this number, or mixing the order invalidated the attempt, and the bank officer would have to reset the dial and start over again.

As he watched the manager and chief cashier began to turn the dials, first one way then another. Either they were a little out of practice, or the combination locks were more than averagely fussy about the numbers coming up exactly without even a slight overshoot tolerance, for they had to dial the numbers several times, giving the fascinated Banner ample opportunity to record the numbers.

Banner watched as the numbers came up, straining to hold his breath without really knowing why. The manager muttered irritably that the combinations would have to be changed or the locks made more forgiving. Finally the manager dialed 69-9-46-10 on the left hand side, and after some delay the cashier managed to dial 25-6-27-7 on the right. The was an almost imperceptible click as the huge locks were released. The manager spun the wheel near the centre of the door and the bolts were drawn back. The door, weighing more than a ton swung silently open, balanced perfectly on it heavily armoured hinges.

After the manager and cashier had deposited the metal box the cashier was holding on to the cash trolley, they stepped out of the vault and went through the ritual of closing the doors again. When their footsteps had died out, Banner inched himself out of the narrow space, not sure if he wanted to sneeze or shout out loud. He suppressed both reactions, scribbled down what he could remember of the numbers on a cigarette packet, turned off the power to the loose cable, and dripping with unseasonable sweat packed up his tools ready to go home, his mind exploding with the significance of what he had just seen.

That night he was not sure that he had correctly remembered both numbers, but to the small group of men that Banner met with in a Fulham pub that night, the figures were of great interest. It was decided he should go back for another look.

Banner got up in the ceiling several times over a period of the next few weeks to be sure that he had got both combinations, as he had to be in two different positions in the ceiling to see both the combinations clearly. In all he spent 17 hours wedged into the ceiling space, watching.

Several nights later, Banner arrived with a miniature but high powered telescope supplied by the ever helpful Freddie Leaf, a container for urine and one for water, and 'stowed away' in the ceiling. The numbers this time were much clearer. Banner made a written note as they clicked past on the dials, first checking one dial, then on the next night the other dial.

All he needed now was the key that opened the door to the vault anteroom. Johnny gave Banner some locks and mechanisms and asked him to check these against the bank ones, to see if that was the same lock type. Johnny also supplied him with an Elastoplast tin filled with a soft waxy substance like plasticine, and showed him how he should take 4 impressions of any key he could lay his hands on. He was to press both sides of the key into the plasticine, then the teeth of the key, and finally its end so that Johnny could gauge what sort of blank to use. He practiced at home with his old door key, left, right, teeth, and end, until it came naturally.

Banner had noticed that when the keyholder went out to lunch he handed the key over to the receptionist to look after. He made a point of chatting up the receptionist: he watched and he waited. Three days later whilst chatting to her, he inadvertently knocked the key off her desk. Quick as a flash, Banner picked up the key, and turning away from her so the girl could not see what he was doing, he pulled out the tin and quickly took the impressions of the key, as he had been taught. Straightening up, he flashed the girl his best smile, apologised, and handed back the key.

Later that evening in the pub, he gave the tin to Johnny Wilde. They now had what they needed.

While Banner was spying out the combinations on the vault doors, Johnny Wilde and Paul Caldwell had been planning some of the other details in their favourite watering hole near where they both lived, the "Cavalier" in Southgate. It was well known to its regulars as a villain's pub, and a fair number of the local cozzers drank there as well.

They fell into conversation with Dave Ranger, someone who was known to have good connections in all the most useful places. It was whispered that he had more than a few cozzers in his pocket as well. He lived just a short way away in one of the best streets in the area: the Lodge had cost him a pretty penny. It was also common knowledge amongst those in the fraternity that he was one of the few fences in London who could rise to the occasion with up to £1 million pounds cash in a few days, if the need arose.

Johnny and Paul certainly thought that the need was going to arise very soon... just as soon as they cracked the Bank of America. Johnny took Dave on one side, "I don't suppose you could handle a serious amount of tom in the near future, if it were to come my way?"

"What do you call serious, a mill?"

'Might be," answered Johnny, "maybe more, but I would want a good price. It'd be all class pieces, no rubbish."

"Yeah, given time, I reckon I could accommodate you on that, what's occurring then? Something big going down?" replied Ranger.

Johnny would not be drawn, but you could see that Dave was more than interested. He was thinking, "if it's to be fenced for more than a million, we are looking at more than £10 million retail value." He knew Johnny Wilde didn't piss about. If Johnny thought he was down for that kind of tom, then he probably was down for it. Dave invited Johnny back to the predecessor of the Circle Club, in Palmers Green, a little after hours drinking club that he owned with a partner. It was a bit more discreet than the Cavalier.

They talked late. Dave said he would make a few preparations, but needed to know when and where. Johnny was deliberately vague, "You don't really expect me to give you all the details, do you?" he joked. They shook hands, and Johnny slipped out the back way — it was long past last orders. Ranger took another mouthful of the neat single malt Scotch that he had cradled between his hands, and began to figure out the odds. Maybe there was more in this than he first thought. He always liked to catch a deal coming and going, so much more satisfying.

Johnny had left Viv at home for the night, he cursed under his breath as he let himself in. He was in for another row — why didn't women understand business? Why couldn't she just accept that in his business you just had to work late.

He was going to have to do some serious thinking about his alibi: Viv was so unpredictable, and vicious when she wanted to be.

Chapter 7 - The Bank yields up its Secrets

The day comes when they are going to do it. They planned to do the job on a Friday night, but when the time came everyone was getting so edgy, that at the last moment Johnny and Jimmy O'Shaughnessy decided to bring it forward and do it on a Thursday night instead. This last minute change also meant less time for anyone to grass.

Freddie Leaf who had masterminded the first attempt wasn't in the country. They knew from Banner, and the first job, that a Group Four Security guard came round checking the doors. Sometimes he did not bother checking the vaults and adjoining corridors, but you could not rely upon that. The security guard's overnight shift included four-hourly checks at 6pm and again at 10pm. They figured that it didn't matter whether it was Thursday or Friday, they still had from 6pm till 10pm to clean the place out.

On the day of the robbery, or to be more technically correct, the burglary, Thursday 24th April 1975, business was normal throughout the day at the Bank. Stewart Banner wasn't in Mayfair, he was doing a normal day's work at the Bank's City branch in Walbrook. He'd almost done his part of the preparation.

At Mayfair the ordinary day staff left the premises as usual. The night computer staff of three came on for the late shift at 5.00 pm. These three, Ian McPherson, Patricia May Hardy and Mohammad Rahman looked forward to a normal night, blissfully unaware of the preparations which had been made earlier that day in Fulham. They were working two floors above the vault, and as on the first raid, were unlikely to hear even quite loud sounds, shut as they were in the air-conditioned computer room, furthest away from the front entrance, with a noisy line-printer hammering away at the Bank's management reports, and the ever present background muzak filling in any other gaps.

Night shifts, even in a bank were sometimes a bit of a lark. If things were a bit slack you could always read the papers, ring up your girlfriend or boyfriend for a long chat, or bring in some junk food and a few beers, as long as the air-conditioned computers kept ticking over, printing out the overnight schedule of reports and statements.

At 5.10 pm the vault was locked by the manager and the alarm set.

Meanwhile I met Johnny early in the afternoon, at his drum in Hedge Lane, Palmers Green, in North London. We had a beer together and I drove him over to Fulham, in south-west London in his car. He was deep in thought, he kept mentally checking over his gear to see that he had everything. He hardly talked, but I could see that his mind was going ten to the dozen. He didn't want to cope with the London traffic, he just wanted to think about the job. Every now and then he would surface and come out with a burst of rapid-fire talk about anything but the job. We threaded our way south through Hornsey, Highgate and Camden, before turning west and then south-west towards Fulham.

We went to Joey Barnum's house off Dawes Road in Fulham, where everyone was to meet and check over the equipment, their individual tasks and every other little detail for the last time. The four of them were sitting there going over things and talking: Johnny, Willy Gavroche, Jimmy, and Paul Caldwell. They each brought kit. Johnny brought the specialist stuff, the keys, and his cutting equipment, while the others brought hammers, chisels, and crowbars to 'cane' the individual safety deposit boxes. They also had another drill with clamps and plenty of drill bits, just in case they needed to drill out any locks. I dropped Johnny off. It was about two o'clock in the afternoon.

Freddie Maiser wasn't there. He comes from the other side of London, the Old Kent Road, beyond Elephant and Castle. Although Paul Caldwell comes from the same area as Johnny, he always drank over this side in Fulham. Paul Caldwell was bringing the blue van which had been specially nicked and re-plated for the job.

The Mayfair Bank Job

It had been made up to look like a cleaner's van, by a reliable guy who worked in Notting Hill. He had even fitted it with a sign, a roof rack and some ladders. Such a van had every reason to be parked outside offices late at night. They all liked the joke, taking the Bank of America to the cleaners.

Because of the parking restrictions no one wanted to get to Mayfair too early. The restrictions came off at six thirty, so they wouldn't be worried about a ticket. Paul first went off to Notting Hill to put his own motor away and pick up the van, then he went to Fulham for the meet. After Paul left Fulham with the van, he went and picked up Freddie Maiser, aiming to arrive at Mayfair at about 5.45pm. He drove it to Mayfair and parked the van up a lane behind the main thoroughfare.

Mickey Jevons made his own way there. Jimmy drove himself to Fulham, and then on by himself to Mayfair. Come to think of it, Freddie might have brought a motor as well, because they had an additional motor in case of emergencies, in case anything went wrong with the van.

As luck would have it, Willy Gavroche got done for parking: just a simple thing you might think. He parked his own motor, a red Ford, in Bruton Place, in Mayfair on a meter a little too early, as an emergency precaution, in case the van did not work, and he needed to get away in a hurry. He took a chance, a chance he should not have taken. That helped the cozzers no end. In fact this ticket was later responsible for tying him into the job. Someone as experienced as him should not have been so stupid. It would have been safer for him to nick a car and leave it there.

You had so many things to look at on a job like this, particularly as we were looking at a getaway from one of the busiest parts of Central London. After all the planning's been done people should know exactly what they are supposed to do, but you still get characters like Willy and Freddie adding just a few little embellishments of their own. Everyone at Joey's was saying "you know your part, don't you?" Of course the answer had to be "yes," even if there were still a few loose ends.

Because of nerves you tended to talk about other things. You go off your topic. You talk about a football match or whatever. You have a few drinks. It all calms the nerves. If it had been a day time thing, or earlier in the morning it would have been a different ball game, you know. You meet up, you go and get tooled up, and then off you go. But when you've got to wait for it to go off, your nerves play up on you.

Even my nerves were a bit on edge, even though I wasn't playing a central part in it, just picking Johnny up, dropping him at Fulham, checking the slaughter, dropping in at Fulham again and picking him up, then dropping him off in Mayfair, and all that. I didn't want to appear nosy, so I didn't ask too many questions. I knew what he was doing. he told me what he was doing, but he also said he didn't know what was likely to be there. There was still going to be an element of improvisation.

I dropped them off at Joey's and where did I go? I went over to Kennington to check the slaughter in South Lambeth Road. I only had to go in and open the gates up, go inside check everything was ready. The slaughter had a yard big enough for two motors to turn in, but with gates that a passing cozzer could not see through. If you climbed over the top of the gates you'd have seen it was a small greengrocers with an open yard like a factory.

I just rummaged around and began running through what I needed to do when the rest of the firm turned up, pretending I was on the job in a way. I was a bit annoyed, a bit choked I wasn't actually on it. Because I was pulled in late anyway, after it was fully planned. I was annoyed that I wasn't that big enough wheel to be pulled in on the job itself. My services weren't needed because I didn't have any special skills. I was in it for a fee, a drink as they say and not a share or a whack.

Someone owned the place we were to use as a slaughter. I had been given the keys to it. The owner gave me a spare set. I told him to make sure that he wasn't around that night and that he had a good alibi. I had already given him good money for using it.

Then, when I was sure everything was in order, I went back and picked Johnny and Willy Gavroche up in Fulham at about four o'clock. Willy had his own car, but he didn't take it to Fulham: he had parked it in Mayfair, then gone to Notting Hill to establish his alibi, and his mate gave him a lift to Fulham. Willy thought he had covered everything, but for the timing on the parking meter. For that he kept his fingers crossed.

If you saw the tack-handed way the others were standing about with different silly little motors, at the time, that they had nicked that day, you would have been surprised. They had their own motors spread about all over the place. They were silly little cars, two of them turned up in one motor, nothing you would mark out as a getaway car, nothing fast or nothing fancy.

The three of us drove up to Mayfair. Johnny was still quiet, bunched up in a tight mental ball, but Willy and I were cracking jokes all the way. We drove along the Fulham Road, through Chelsea, into Brompton Road and Knightsbridge. We went through the underpass at Hyde Park Corner and into Piccadilly. As we passed the posh shops and hotels Willy said "I'll have a piece of that." We all agreed that more than a few occupants of Mayfair were very soon going to be rather upset and short of a few of their trinkets.

Into Davies Street via Berkeley Square, we passed the Bank of America on our left, "just to see if it was still there." Willy couldn't help giving it a friendly wave. We doubled back to the small cafe in Mount Street where we had agreed to meet. I can remember it was a little hole in the wall cafe. There was an entrance behind it where you could get sandwiches and a cup of tea. That's where I left them. I think, if I remember correctly it was shortly after quarter to five o'clock. It was light. The journey had taken 45 minutes, but could easily have taken over an hour, if there was a traffic screw-up: better safe than sorry.

I took Johnny to a side turning, and he told me they had the van parked up there. Instead of setting off immediately as planned I parked the car round the corner on a meter and cautiously walked back to the Bank.

When all the team had arrived, including Mickey Jevons, they had a quick cuppa. They strolled up Davies Street to Three Kings Yard in ones and twos like men going to work the late shift. They took their tools with then in holdalls, crow bars, hammers, and jemmies, because they hadn't have time or the opportunity to key up all the locks.

The Bank of America premises went from Davies Street through a whole block, as do many of the businesses in that part of Mayfair, onto the T-shaped service lane called Three Kings Yard. The Bank's back door opened on to the top left arm of the 'T,' while the foot of the 'T' met Davies Street a short distance from the front door of the Bank. The lane also serviced the back of the Canadian Embassy, the Italian Embassy, and other businesses.

I wondered briefly what would happen if the police turned up and closed off the mouth of Three King's Yard before they were able to escape. Caught like rats in a trap. I brushed the thought from my mind and concentrated on the job in hand. They weren't going to get caught, it would be easier than last time: just a stroll. Knowing the combinations would mean no heavy gear, no drilling, and no noise. The 'speed' (methedrine) we had all taken at Fulham coursed through my veins, and the warm certainty of a successful job replaced the fleeting fear.

At 5.00 pm Banner finished working at the other branch of the bank in Walbrook in the City of London. He had struck up a friendship with an elderly bank messenger of impeccable character called Percy Woods, and had as on previous evenings, arranged to take him home. Woods had previously worked in the early seventies for another foreign bank, an Australian bank I think, near Berkeley Square and had only a few years to go to his retirement. It was a comfortable arrangement and one which on this evening gave Banner an excellent alibi.

Banner phoned Woods at the Davies Street branch, from where he was working at Walbrook, to confirm that he would indeed be picking him up. Banner left the Walbrook branch and arrived at Davies Street at 5.40 pm. He parked in Three Kings Yard away from the ever present threat of the voracious central London parking wardens. He greeted Wood and asked him to sit in his car while he popped into the bank, he casually lied "I may have left my drill downstairs in the vault. I must just go and see if I left my tools behind."

He went downstairs to the vault to see if anybody was working late in that area. He flicked the switch he had specially installed to cut the power to the alarm system. He returned to the car and said "I must see if I have left it in the computer room." He went up to the computer room, popping his head into the banking hall as he went to check if there was any late workers still cashing up. The banking hall was deserted. He turned the muzak up.

Before he and Wood drove off towards Battersea, where Banner lived with his parents, he flashed his headlights twice to signal the rest of the team who had taken up their positions and were waiting further down Three Kings Yard for Banner's all clear. In the dusk several heads nodded, and waited for Banner's car to disappear round the corner and out of King's Yard before moving towards the rear of the Bank.

The Group Four Security guard finished his check and drove off. It was 6.05 pm. Now in they went, Johnny went in first. Using the key he had cut months previously, he opened the back gate. He went through the gate, and opened the door, just as if he was reporting for work. Willy was close on his heels, then Paul, Mickey Jevons and Freddie, in rapid succession. The back entrance was ideal to load the van and the motors. They were all 'turtled up' with gloves, but no masks so as not to arouse suspicion.

Four lookouts slipped silently into position, one at the top of the 'T' of Three King's Yard where he could see both the back of the Bank and the entrance to the Yard. Another lounged about near the corner of Davies Street and Grosvenor Street, where he had a clear view of both Streets and the entrance to the front Bank. There was no way the cozzers could reach the bank without one of these lookouts spotting them. The third came into the Bank, and going up the stairs from the basement crouched at their top, near where they entered the banking hall. He could see anything happening in the banking hall, as well as being able to watch the street through the vertical blinds. The fourth lookout took up the same position on the other staircase where he could see anyone coming down the interior staircase from the computer room above, and watch the other side of the banking hall.

I watched them till the last had closed the door. I walked back to where I had left Johnny's motor, turned it around, and I'm out of there. I'm on my way to the slaughter.

My next job is to make sure the slaughter is open. They were doing the business. Now I have to wait in the slaughter down in Kennington, I don't know how long they'll be, they reckon they will be 6 hours. It turned out it was a bit longer than that: it felt like forever. I don't know what's happening their end, and they can't get in touch with me. You can't just phone up and ask.

Plenty of time. Sunset was at 7.10 pm, but by the time I reached Kennington in the slow peak hour traffic the sun was obscured by buildings and dusk was settling rapidly. I always fancied that I had one of the worst jobs, I was sitting waiting at the other end, waiting for them to turn up: none of the excitement, none of the adrenaline, but just the waiting and the stomach churning. It was not even safer having to wait, because Old Bill doesn't always pounce immediately they tumble a raid. Sometimes they just follow the participants to see where they're going. They always like to widen their net a bit, you know, it's like that.

In the early '70s, people started to use walkie-talkies for jobs, instead of having a lookout, or a 'dog-eye.' Most people got away with it. I was using walkie-talkies in 1969. Then I heard about people listening in, but when the CB's came out in about 1976, illegally, we used to use them to get in contact with each other.

We used to go and call our mates on the channels, the CBs would

The Mayfair Bank Job

go up to 23 channels or something, and just briefly talk to make a meeting at "the little green bottle shop," meaning some such prearranged pub. Those CBs seemed to be the answer to everything, you know what I mean? They always used to laugh at me because I used to talk in this American accent, "Yeah, howdy good buddy, yeah Roger." A lot of meetings, and a few jobs, were organised that way.

It would have been useful to have a walkie-talkie on this job and stay in touch with the rest of the team in the Bank. Even the lookout inside the bank could have used one to talk with the rest in the vault. Remember that the first attempt failed because the lookout couldn't be heard over the din of the drills and so stupidly turned the power off. However we didn't have walkie-talkies because it would be crazy to allow the whole world to listen in on what we were doing. Even if we had spoken in code, with the right equipment the police could close in on you tracking your transmissions, although in those days, not everybody knew that.

Everything had been worked out in detail. The team had gone in the gate round the back of the Bank of America, a little wooden gate with a Yale lock that enters directly into the back of the building. The alarms were turned off, Banner had made sure the alarms were no longer supplied with electricity, and just to be sure the needle on the voice alarm had been removed. Johnny had made the keys, including the Yale key to open the gate which is the first hard obstacle to anybody entering the Bank from the back. Because they were out in the open, it had to work first time — there could be no standing round fiddling with it.

Johnny also had to make a key for the back door. The job was planned as a complete walk-in. When he was making that key, even Johnny had to go back two or three times to check that his keys worked properly.

Before the job, I went over there once with Johnny one evening. Without any prior warning he just stopped near the Bank and said matter of factually, "I've just got to pop up here." He went up Three King's Yard, and checked his keys were working, and he even left the gate open. I vaguely remember seeing a fire escape, because you can't help being nosey can you? He was really unassuming about his work and everything looked matter of fact with him. It was just a wooden door, but it obviously had a hefty security lock on it because he had a bit of trouble with that one. It wasn't a two minute job to do that key, but on the night itself it opened as smooth as silk.

Because Johnny could not get an original key to cut from, the key was made from a plastic hairbrush, like the bristles from a broom, designed to still open the tumblers even if it wasn't exactly the right shape. To make such a skeleton key, he used to get a key, an ordinary Yale key, and cut the teeth off. On to the spine of the key Johnny would glue bristles with superglue, sticking upwards. He then shaped special soft metal that was brought in from France, it was not ordinary metal, but on this occasion Johnny used bristles.

So they gained entry into the back gate, slid the bolt, opened the door security lock, passed through the door in the back, and down the stairs to the by now familiar vault antechamber. They didn't look round upstairs in the computer room at all. They made their way straight down to the vault and started the business. They gingerly checked the alarm cupboard to make sure that Banner had indeed done his part and cut the alarm power. Everything seemed OK.

Johnny worked his magic on the outer doors of the vault area, and they passed through like ghosts, closing them behind them. They could still see the stairs through a security glass panel, which was used by the clerk admitting customers to the vault during the day. Mickey took up his position there, watching to see if anyone came down the stairs. Once they got into the safety deposit area they knew the combinations to the vault door.

It was the work of about four minutes to dial each code carefully, praying that the codes had not been changed. Johnny, who probably had the steadiest nerves, carefully turned the dial on the left, stopping on 69. Willy sniggered quietly to himself. Johnny turned the dial in the opposite direction to 9, then back to 46. They all held their breath as the dial was turned in the opposite direction to 10. There was no click. "Did you do it?" whispered Freddie, grabbing for the door.

Johnny said nothing, but brushed Freddie's hand away and turned his attention to the right hand dial. Urged on by the others, and feeling just a little cocky, Johnny started to dial the numbers for the right hand dial. First 25, then back to 6 then 27. The dial registered 28 but Johnny turned it back to 7. Again no click, but he wasn't expecting one. He gingerly fingered the hand wheel which withdraws the bolts, but it was unyielding.

Paul Caldwell, who hadn't taken any part so far swore under his breath, but before Freddie could angrily demand "what's going on?" Johnny held up his hand and cut him short. He realised that he had overshot the mark on the third turn, and scrambling the tumblers with a swift full turn to the right, he carefully dialed 25-6-27-7 again, taking care to stop precisely on the required digits. Again there was no click from the precision ground lock, but Johnny knew that when he grabbed the hand wheel it would turn easily, withdrawing the array of bolts from their secure sockets in the surrounding steel frame.

Johnny hesitated for effect and then turned the wheel and leant back. The huge door opened with a slight sigh of displaced air passing into the vault. The floor plate dropped into place automatically. The men exchanged glances which said more than words, Freddie suppressed a strong desire to punch the air, and they all walked into the vault. Even Mickey left his lookout position to have a look at the largest prize any of them had ever seen.

Chapter 8 - The Vault

The vault extended in both directions, every wall covered with hundreds of shiny metal doors, each with sizeable but vulnerable hinges and two sturdy looking keyholes. They did not know it at the time, but there were a massive 600 safety deposit boxes round the walls of the vault whose floor area covered 340 square feet. Each wall of boxes was just over 18 foot long. These safety deposit boxes ranged in size from 4" by 8", with a depth of 19", big enough for documents, jewellery and some currency, through larger boxes of 8" by 8" by 19" deep, up to locker size which were used by the bank itself and those of its customers with bulky objects d'art or really sizeable stashes. The later were much harder to open, and tended to be at floor level.

The ceiling and the few pieces of spare wall were lined with steel panels, and the floor was carpeted. A small desk, chair and key cage made up the minimal furniture inside the vault. High up on one wall was a clock, and just outside the vault door were several private viewing cubicles for the use of customers who wanted to empty or fill their boxes away from prying eyes.

Once in the vault, there was no way the team could have secured keys for the hundreds of private boxes: even the bank did not have these. Each box was secured by two keys, a bank master key and a key belonging to the box holder. Both keys had to be present to open the box. It had to be all hammer and chisel, lever and bash, canning the safety deposit boxes open with crow bars. This did not have the finesse of Johnny's work, but it required time and strength. Each man took in his working bag with his tools.

Like all safe deposits vaults, they assumed this one did not include the working cash of the bank, just the bundles of cash secreted by their trusting customers, not the money they deposited in their accounts, but the rainy day money in thick cash bundles.

But laying on a trolley just inside the door was the bank's own cash from the tills upstairs. They didn't know it at the time, but this trolley alone held £143,245.28p plus a further US$235,352, travelers cheques, and money orders. They deliberately missed one box which contained over £1 million in travelers cheques, much to the smug satisfaction of the Bank. They left the cheques and money orders, because they knew they would have trouble cashing them. The cash however went straight into a bag.

Paul opened his holdall and dumped the empty post office bags on the desk. He draped one over the back of the chair while the rest of the team unzipped their holdalls, and started testing their jemmies on the nearest box that took their fancy. The first door to break open was greeted by a low, "fuck me," and then a whistle as the deed box inside yielded to a practiced wrench of the crowbar. Inside was twenty or thirty neat packets of brand new £20 notes, and a stack of plastic cylinders the size of Smarties tubes. Each tube contained a neat row of Krugerrands, each worth something like £200 each. Each tube, heavier than lead, weighed in at roughly £10,000.

Like a feeding frenzy the others set to work bashing and levering at the other boxes. Some of the bigger boxes required two men each working a crowbar to cane them open. Inside each locker was a slide out box that was often padlocked with a padlock belonging to the box holder, but here the hasps gave way to one quick action with a jemmy. Even so, it was taking between 5 and 10 minutes to break open each box.

Johnny carefully drilled a few redundant holes into the doors near the locks, so that the police would think that the vault door was opened that way, rather than by using the combination numbers. This was designed to throw suspicion off Banner. It was assumed that the police would be as careless as they had on the first raid, and not grill Banner. On the bigger safety deposit boxes Johnny also attempted to use the drill, hoping to find a much bigger prize inside.

The Mayfair Bank Job

Banner had specially asked them to break up the false ceiling just outside the vault door to destroy any traces of his night long vigils, but they were far too busy to do that.

Every now and then one of them would check with the lookout on the stairs, whilst the others worked their way randomly round the room, tackling the boxes at waist height first, getting in each other's way. They figured they had a clear four hours till the next visit by the Group Four Security guard. They thought they would be finished by then, but they hadn't reckoned on finding close to 600 safety deposit boxes. What a pity to waste the opportunity.

They figured that if they had not finished by 10 pm they would have to go. The guard probably only wanted to rattle a few doors and check the locks, but it was not worth taking a chance. They couldn't after all lock themselves in the vault until he had passed. After the 10.00 pm visit, they figured they had another clear four hours till 2.00 am the next morning, but they thought they would not press their luck, and be well away before then. They were originally quite confident about how long they would be in the vault, but they seriously underestimated the number of boxes and the time it took to break open each one.

Soon the floor was covered with papers and empty metal boxes. The relatively small space, the size of an average living room (18 x 18 feet) was beginning to look as if a bomb had hit it. Their plans to work their way through the vault systematically broke down as each man began opening whatever box door came to hand. Some were empty, some were jammed packed: there did not seem to be a pattern.

They were popping the stuff into the stack of mailbags that they brought with them — too late they realised how difficult it is to both hold a bag open and shake a metal box into it. The usable stuff, the jewellery, the tiaras, the rings and necklaces, and the bags of loose diamonds were dropped into bags willy-nilly with the wads of notes in various currencies and the tubes of Krugerrands — time enough to sort this out when they reached the slaughter.

Willy couldn't resist a laugh — he kept holding up the things he found, the pictures of worn and drooping old men with pert breasted young ladies in high heels, stockings and not much else, the whips and manacles. What they said about the English upper class was more than amply confirmed by the contents of these previously most secret boxes. More sinisterly they found several pistols, even a Luger automatic and a Mauser machine pistol. Freddie was more than interested in these trophies, taking time off to test their actions. They worked steadily for an hour before they stopped and had tea and sandwiches.

Someone would say "do you want a cup of tea?" Willy would turn, hold up his latest ridiculous prize, and say "fuck off, what do you think this is a picnic?", and then they'd all laugh. It's nerves that's doing that, but the jokes were much healthier than tempers flaring.

You'd be surprised. Because of the way things are, work was not done as quickly as possible, but in a jokey way that had the unreal atmosphere of a picnic in a rifled Aladdin's cave. The speed, the methedrine, certainly enhanced that unreal feeling, whilst providing more energy than by now aching muscles wanted to provide. They worked hard, but could not resist stopping and savouring the madness of it all. You tend to relax at certain points on a job when you think "we're all right, nothing can stop us now." They were in, and nobody was going to stop them. They could see that they were literally shoveling millions into those rapidly expanding bags.

The team continued their work steadily caning open the boxes of the individual safety deposit boxes with crowbars and jemmies.

Without warning the raid took what a newspaper later described with some exaggeration as 'a violent turn.' In fact the events of that evening were almost inevitable, as the computer staff moved freely about the offices of the bank as they had done during the first raid. Other gangs might have secured all the staff at the beginning of the raid, but we did not attempt to do so, as it was supposed to be a burglary.

The Mayfair Bank Job

Bear in mind the whole essence of the Bank of America job was that it was supposed to be a burglary, not a robbery. No guns, no force, no violence, just stealing quietly in and just as quietly out again.

Now if you can imagine the building, there is a metal staircase, a fire escape, at the back of the building. Unbeknown to anybody, not even Banner realised that, there was a door which went out to the fire escape, up one end, and then up to where there was another office.

The other office was not even in the Bank building. It was part of the next adjacent street number, but used by the Bank's computer staff. There was a communal staircase which served both street numbers.

Nobody really thought that anybody was working late, it was Thursday night and although they knew there were computer rooms on the first floor, they were well tucked up in their air-conditioned cocoon, and they weren't really a problem. We knew we could even use a high speed drill without disturbing them. In fact the *Times* next day got the facts a little out of perspective and reported that "the raiders took the cash, in pounds and dollars, after drilling into a safe. Later they broke into private safe deposits."

At 7.15 pm, in the middle of the operation, one of the computer staff came downstairs from the first floor to the banking hall to make a telephone call. Perhaps he didn't want to log a call on his own phone extension upstairs, who knows.

The lookout on the stairs from the basement to the ground floor saw the computer operator and went downstairs to warn the rest. Something made Freddie go back to the vault anteroom and look through the glass panel. He waved everyone to stop making a noise. Freddie went upstairs to join the lookout: they were watching the staff member come down into the room. You would have assumed it was a security guard, wouldn't you? No other staff had any reason to come down there.

Well, when he went to the phone, we assumed he was calling the police. We assumed that he'd either seen something or heard something. He dialed 3 numbers, what would you think now? Definitely the police, it's got to be '999' hasn't it. They couldn't see what he was doing, they just went "oh shit." The two moved across the floor as if their lives depended on it: they claimed him, got hold of him, on the third number before he got it through. The look of terror on his face was comical.

He just stood there holding the phone in his hand, totally gobsmacked. Suddenly from the phone handset came the strains of "Love, Love Me Do." Can you believe it, he was ringing dial-a-disc to check the latest top of the pops. Whatever it was, he didn't know anything about it till then grabbed him. Freddie jumped him, waving a gun about and holding it to his head, like he was in the movies. The operator was frightened, his bottle went. Ian McPherson was just 19 and new to the job of computer operator. They tied him up with tape. They didn't gag him, they just said "keep quiet, and we won't need none of that." He couldn't even speak, he just nodded, trying to breathe.

When he was able to speak, he revealed that one of the other computer staff, Mohammad Rahman, was upstairs and would miss him if he did not return, so two of the team including Mickey went upstairs to claim him. There was also an old girl up there, the supervisor Patricia Hardy. They'd got to claim her too. They reached the first floor, and started into the room on hands and knees so as not to be seen, especially from the offices opposite. In a few seconds Mickey and Jimmy brought down both of them with no fuss. Afterwards they were all laughing about it. "Don't fucking believe it — where has he come from?"

This was the only hiccup, but it turned a really neat burglary into a robbery. Later the Crown was to charge one of the participants with the sample robbery of these three members of staff in preference to simply a charge of burglary against the Bank.

Mickey Jevons took them to the kitchen downstairs in the basement at the same level as the vault, where he made them a cup of tea to calm their nerves, and gave them a couple of biscuits! Then he tied up the other two. Nice and firm but not painful. No harm, and no one there was violent. They removed the glasses that two of the staff were wearing, so that they could not get a good look at their temporary captors. In fact the idea was suggested by the youngest of the operators. The only thing that went wrong was that Freddie had a gun, worse still he had produced it in front of witnesses. Nobody knew he had a gun: if he had just kept it in his pocket.

Except for one of the team, who had brought a balaclava, they weren't masked up. The staff could have identified Freddie Maiser and a few of the others later in court, except Freddie was never brought to court over it. The *Times* on the 26 April 1975 said that the burglars wore balaclava masks. The three witnesses decided that for their own safety they should report that the burglars all wore masks.

The *Times* the next day reported that "the gang who wore hoods held the staff at gunpoint and tied them up with flex and adhesive tape." There was no intention to do anyone any harm, because if anybody got nicked, you were nicked for burglary, you were not nicked for anything else, no gelignite, no arms, no nothing. You would hold your hand up to burglary rather than get something more serious pinned on you, you're in there simply burgling. That was the idea, pure and simple. Anyway, then this little thing came out, and there was the gun, you have had it.

That's why they were a bit choked up with Freddie and his gun. For a second or two they thought he was going to shoot the fella. The team had always said they would not carry firearms, so that in case they were caught their maximum sentences would be much lower. That Freddie decided to carry a gun, was purely his decision, a decision that the rest of the team lived to regret.

This messing round with the staff took longer than they realised. A rougher bunch might have just bundled them up and got on with the job, but they calmed them down and gave them tea instead. In the time they had left they only opened 97 boxes of which only 89 boxes were actually rented with contents, a mere 16% of the total 600 boxes present.

They knew what they had was so much that they didn't need to do them all. They wanted to get out before anything else went wrong, before their captives were missed. Somebody was going to be looking for them sooner or later. They lost almost 40 minutes arguing over the staff. One man stayed with them in the kitchen, straining his ears for any sign that they had been missed.

At 9.35 pm they stopped work. They decided not to wait for the Group Four Security guard to come by. He in fact later arrived at 10.07 pm. They moved the by now full bags up to just inside the back door, and soon after started loading them into the van. Hand to hand they moved quickly. It nearly filled the van up so there must have been about twenty to twenty-five big bags. The van's floor was completely covered and they had started to bank the bags up when one of the gang thought they saw some movement further down Three Kings Yard. It could have been a wino or a derelict sifting about in the high class piles of rubbish or it could have been Old Bill taking up positions.

They retreated inside, held a hurried conference, some wanting to finish the job, others wanting to make a break for it. They decided that enough was enough. Freddie was beginning to brandish his gun again, "they have seen our faces" he whined. Johnny wanted to release the captives, he figured they were too scared to do anything, after all it was not their money. Johnny at least wanted to make a phone call. Heated words were exchanged. Finally they checked the three night staff were still bound, banking on the visit from the Group Four Security guard to release then, and left them in the kitchen. They took one more look round the vault at all those seductively closed little steel doors, figured that they had little enough room left in the van anyway, and then scarpered.

Chapter 9 - The Slaughter

Freddie, for reasons of his own, drove off by himself, planning to collect his share much later. It wasn't until much later that we heard what he had in his pocket. He was not exactly top of everybody's hit parade so we didn't ask him why. Willy and Johnny, exhausted after a hard night's work, but not yet coming down from the speed, piled into another car, while Mickey Jevons drove the van by himself. Paul and Jimmy followed by a different route in another car. Jimmy drove north from Davies Street, across Oxford Street, turned left, up Gloucester Street, left along George Street and finally stopped near a block of flats in Harroby Street. He left Paul in the car and dashed upstairs, for few minutes, then after checking the coast was clear set off southwards for the slaughter.

They all trusted Mickey Jevons to arrive at the slaughter with a car that had been nicked a few weeks before. They were plated up, filled, tuned, serviced and had everything done: someone in Notting Hill was in for a drink for supplying them. They were proper motors: there was nothing about them to suggest to the police to give them a pull. Of course there was another car with the same number plate floating about somewhere, but only a million to one chance of bumping in to it.

Back at the slaughter I was waiting and wondering what had happened. It seemed like an eternity. I mean, what do you do to pass the time, try and read, walk about a bit? I kept going to the gate to see if they had arrived. I didn't want to do much opening and shutting the gate in case anyone saw me. I popped over to the pub opposite, the Canton, but I couldn't really settle down to a pint: I kept looking out the window. At closing time I went back to the slaughter and just lurked around, hoping that I would see familiar faces and not the Old Bill. After all what had I done? So far nothing.

All of a sudden they turned up. It was pretty close to eleven thirty: I reckoned I had been sitting around for ages. When they came back they were full of it. You can imagine them just bursting when they pulled in, punching the sky and shouting "yes." Johnny and Willy arrived first in one of the 'moody' motors. Even Johnny was over the moon: perhaps more than any of us he knew the value of what they had got.

I opened the gates, and closed then pretty sharpish behind the blue van as soon as Mickey arrived. The others came in at different times, but all within the space of three or four hours, just to cover themselves.

Some of them might have called in on sweethearts, others needed to establish their alibis as close to the time of the raid as they could. Perhaps one or two wanted to be sure that the Old Bill hadn't tailed them before returning to the slaughter.

Yet others might have had put a little something in their pockets that needed emptying. Although it was supposed to be an equal share-out, the temptation to put a little something in your pocket or your sock tops was overwhelming. What happened if the others got a pull from the police? A little something in the pocket then at least made the whole night's work worthwhile.

When they came back they emptied everything out on the floor of the slaughter, bag after bag was opened and flapped free of its contents. Willy Gavroche was so funny. The comical things they were saying and doing. They all were pretty high. "It was a doddle, a pint of piss."

It was really because that's the point when the tension gets released. They had been like wound up springs for the last seven hours, or longer. It's when you've got to the slaughter, your doors are shut tight, there is no pursuit, and you know you're all right, that's when you can really relax.

When you do a bit of work, say you're holding up a security van, it's not until you've got your motor tucked away with your money there that you know that you can relax. You know the chances are you might get a visit from the cozzers, if you're a really active person and ever so well known by the police, that you might get a visit that evening even. The police knocking on your door and all that is part of the game, but apart from that you can then relax.

Despite the fact that most of the papers were left on the floor of the vault we found we still had a lot of papers. There were more than a few relating to MPs and other familiar faces from business, show business and funny business. Speaking about funny business, there was a lot of papers which looked like dossiers and lists of names, and a lot of political papers in there as well.

Nobody really understood them. Nobody was really interested. The political involvement was brought out quite strongly later during the trial. We glanced at them, but we didn't want to get mixed up in anything really crooked like that: all the papers were burnt.

The CIA had obviously used the vault, presumably for papers too sensitive to store in the strong-room at their own US Embassy in Grosvenor Square, two blocks away. None of it meant very much to any of us, but the files tied with different coloured ribbons, with confidential stamps on them obviously meant a lot to somebody. A lot of the stuff seemed to be about the private lives of their own staff.

The gang left some of this stuff on the floor of the vault for the benefit of the police. I don't know if the police took advantage of it, but they must have had a good laugh over some of the photos. In amongst the material wrenched from the individual safe deposit boxes was a file of papers and photos which were obviously still being used for blackmail. The team very thoughtfully left this behind for the attention of the police, possibly to the great relief of the victim, a fairly prominent publicly known figure.

Although they threw piles of papers on the floor, there were still many papers in the bags. There were photos of geezers and birds, and plenty of whips: they even had photos of people on a rack. We were all laughing about it. Willy was saying "can we get their addresses and go round to see em?" And things like that because he is one of those people, a born a comic.

When they were taking documents out of the boxes, some of them were in special bags. Some of it we threw out, but in amongst the papers we sometimes found a prize like a bag of gold or diamonds, there were a lot of diamonds. There were thousands upon thousands of Krugerrands. They were a very popular hedge against inflation in the early seventies. Many of these Krugerrands from this vault raid showed up again in the nineteen eighties in connection with one of the apparent gold VAT scams, but more of that later.

After we had brought in all the bags there was an argument about some of the bags. They were supposed to have loaded all of the bags into one van. But I think that one or two bags may have found their way into the odd car boot. Two bags of mainly jewellery went missing between the Bank and the slaughter. Everyone was just a bit too hyper to notice, especially when it came to the last minute loading in Three Kings Yard. There was only one van that pulled up with the gear at the slaughter, and there wasn't that long between their arrival times, within about half an hour of each other.

But with a bit of planning its marvelous what you can do with half an hour, especially when its late at night and the roads are very empty.

We did say at the time, some of them could have had "lumpy socks." Meaning that they could have slipped off to their girlfriends or their wives and dropped some of their stuff. But when they came in they all shook hands — I'll never forget it.

They all went "blinding, absolute beaut, fucking beaut, can't knock it, went like a dream." Then on a sorrier note, "pity about Freddie," because that was the only bad thing about that robbery that had not gone like a dream was Freddie Maiser and his bit of bad news.

Nobody knew Freddie had a gun on him. When he pulled a gun out on that fella that came down to make a phone call, the rest of the team couldn't believe their eyes. They had all agreed that what they were doing was a burglary, not an aggravated burglary or a 'stick your hands up' robbery. Mind you there was more than enough pistols to go around in the boxes themselves.

Nobody wanted to do all that extra time if they got caught. They all reckoned that if they got done, then they could do a few to five years no problem — definitely worth the night's swag. But with the gun they were looking at a lot more porridge. Apart from that they were over the moon with themselves. Johnny had to sort out some stuff for Freddie Maiser for the next day, because he wasn't at the slaughter, which is just as well considering how they all felt about him.

Then we unloaded the motor. They were all giggling and mucking about. I'm pulling sacks out of the motor. There wasn't just sacks in there. There was brief cases, steel boxes, cardboard boxes and holdalls full of gear. None had their lids on right. I was pulling them out and putting them down. They emptied out the sacks and I was mesmerised by a lot of it. I've got to be honest with you. They were doing silly things like picking up crowns, tiaras, and putting them on their heads, mucking about. You've never seen so many Krugerrands. They were in tubes and weighed a ton!

They started bringing in the bags, often dragging them because of the weight. They would untie them, and upend them, if you saw all the shit you would not have believed it, it was worth a fortune. On the floor there was a mass of sparkling jewellery, tiaras, necklaces, chains, brooches, and loose stones in amongst the coins, all this paperwork, bonds and wads of notes. I'm not even counting the paper: I don't know anything about bonds, I don't know anything about stocks and shares. Mickey was interested but I didn't understand it, it was just bits of paper to me and they left half of them on the floor, and what they didn't leave, I burned. They could not be used, as the police would be able to trace them.

I thought they were never going to stop coming in with these bags crammed with stuff. The gold, the jewellery, and the money had to be sorted and separated. We were there till early Friday morning. It took us another five hours to sort it out, roughly. I'm talking about really roughly, They counted the money, but shared the jewellery out using greengrocer's scales to divide it by weight. They split it into eight roughly equal piles, and drew lots for which pile each was to have. The main men all had equal shares. They didn't have all the cash to cut up between them, because there was a lot of expenses for the motors, the slaughter and for this, that and the other. They ended up taking home £800,000 in cash each.

The balance was left with Johnny and Paul to pay the other people who were involved in their different roles since the beginning for getting various things and carrying out various services.

You can imagine the scene at the slaughter: twenty to thirty mailbags full and tipped out on the floor, the pile covering most of the floor to the depth of a desk. An awful lot to sort through, not like simply splitting up the cash proceeds of a robbery. With time pressing and the ever present chance of the police arriving uninvited, the division into roughly 'equal' piles was carried out with more speed than accuracy. The division of a much smaller amount of money by the Great Train Robbers in 1963 took considerably longer.

How do you think the team felt when in amongst the very much more valuable papers turned out on to the threadbare carpet of the slaughter was just on eight million pounds in cash alone, three times the total amount stolen in the Great Train Robbery.

They knew there was a lot of money there, in any safety deposit you're going to get large amounts of money. Nobody guessed that it would be eight million pounds in cash. But this was just the beginning.

If you can imagine someone coming into the room with many mail bags full of jewellery, and then tipping it on the floor, then you've a got a pile the size of an average desk, just of jewellery.

I'm not exaggerating, but there was a rug about 12' x 6," and it had all round the outside of it piles of money, English, German Deutschmarks, dollars from all over the world, and equally down one side was tubes of Krugerrands, tubes and tubes, you've never seen so many Krugerrands and that was just on this one rug.

So there are eight main people on this job entitled to a whack, while everybody else has got to get paid off drinks, fixed amounts, for supplying cars and driving or who had done their bit beforehand, like Banner, or supplying different pieces of what we needed like sacks.

That was a much bigger pile than the Great Train robbery. The Great Train robbery was only £2.6 million. In this pile here was £26 million, altogether in currency, gold, silver and jewellery.

My job was to bag up the shit, but there was an argument, there was a bad argument about the money, especially the foreign currency. You know how they divvied it up? They should have had roughly £800,000 each in cash alone, and Paul and Johnny were going to take the rest of the excess and whatever was left they were going to divvy up.

Young Freddie said he wasn't having that, "you're at it you two."

Johnny and Willy divided the money into eight roughly equal piles and they then said to the others "which one do you want?" It's as fair a way to divide anything in a hurry. One party does the division, the other party does the choosing: nobody can cheat. When it came to the jewellery, nobody had valued anything, nobody knows what's there, or what its really worth. You might finish up with a pile of junk, you didn't know.

Even I was excited, though my money wasn't going to be anywhere near that amount, I was excited for them. Johnny was the coolest one out of all us. He said "I'll tell you what I'll do, I will give you £10,000 each for all your tom, your jewellery and I'll dispose of the lot."

Those who were there all agreed to that. To this day nobody knows what happened or how it got fenced. Chances are it was worth a lot more than £10,000 per pile, but Johnny offered to take the risk, and they all accepted his offer, except Freddie who was not at the slaughter.

For them no jewellery meant no hassle. With £800,000 in cash you didn't need to worry, you didn't need to get caught with an identifiable piece of jewellery which could land you straight in jail.

Freddie was still not happy. Now bear in mind, Freddie's got a gun, so everybody is a little bit skeptical of Freddie, because he's a nutter anyway. He comes from a nutty family and he ain't behind the door himself for being a bit nutty. So he's going "I'm still not happy." He's walking out the door and arguing about money.

Johnny said to him "Why don't you fucking shut up, you've got enough money on you now, there's nobody gonna do you out of nothing. I'll get an accountant, you fucking idiot, and put everything down in the book, do you want me to do that?"

And with that, we all laughed, I mean, the thought of getting an accountant to say what he had done with the 2 million pound that was over, and with the jewellery which nobody could value was ridiculous. I mean, everybody sat there with so much money in front of them.

Who was going to bother working out exchange rates for US dollars or Deutschemark? I was laughing to myself, how could we know there's 14 Deutschemarks to a so many dollars, or whatever? Nobody thought to buy a "Financial Times", even if we did think to bring a calculator.

I don't know, but Freddie, he's thinking to himself, "I wonder whether they're having me over, there may be $3 to the £1 instead of $2 or vice versa," do you know what I mean? "Or there may be only so many Guilders in the pound, and Krugerrands may be worth $250, but maybe they ain't." With Freddie, even having the "Financial Times" handy might not have sorted the situation.

Exactly, but can you imagine the turmoil it caused because they knew there was plenty of money down there in the vault, but they never thought of working out foreign currency, or travelers cheques, or even jewellery. Everybody who got paid off, got paid off in sterling, except the 4 main men, Johnny, Willy and Jimmy and Mickey. They're the ones who said "I'll take dollars, I don't mind, I don't mind Escudos, or whatever it was there."

The next problem was tucking all that money into a bag. They though their holdalls plus a mailbag or two each would do the trick. It wouldn't. Have you ever seen what that kind of money looks like? And it's not neatly folded money, it's not neatly packed with elastic bands around it, and all that. I mean they're stuffing them in, but when they get it out, wherever they have got to go, it has all got to be sorted again.

It was a ridiculous scene, they were all struggling out the door one by one and jumping in motors and driving off, some of them having trouble carrying their lolly.

There was a crooked cab company involved in the job as well. It had to ferry all the blokes from the slaughter in South Lambeth Road, Kennington to wherever they wanted to go. They were not going to drive themselves. Nobody in his right mind would bring his own motor within three miles of the slaughter, because the cozzers could check the number plates against known talent in the robbery game.

They had their own motors tucked away in all the sleazy places where they wanted them. Paul for example had left his car at Notting Hill, Willy left his in Mayfair, just in case. For the others, one cab might go to Catford, one cab might go to Streatham, one cab might go to Clapham, one cab might go to Croydon. But that's the way they wanted it, and that was the way it was all worked out, each one got his own cab, but all the cabs had been pre-ordered from the same bent company. Obviously their own cars were on route to wherever they were going to stash their gear. When it came to leaving the slaughter, each left by himself. One by one away they all went. By then it was almost 5 am Friday morning.

One of them headed for home and then on to the London Silver Vaults in Chancery Lane where he was going to keep his gear. Amazing

The Mayfair Bank Job

isn't it, they just knocked over a safe deposit vault, yet he is prepared to trust his money to another one, and a much older one at that.

Meanwhile, I got the furnace fired up, and started feeding it. We took no chances, if we didn't immediately recognise something, or anything looked a bit iffy, straight into the furnace it went. I had to burn all the papers, the spare bags, and anything else that might link us to the raid, a pity, but it had to be done. Because there was too many ashes being generated, because the neighbours might have noticed the smoke, and because there was so much to do, I had to burn the balance later that day. There wasn't half some paper work to do away with.

Johnny was left. I helped Johnny put all of his stuff into bags and sacks, mailbags, grey plastic ones. But I'm telling you, there must have been almost 16 bags for Johnny's gear which by now included all the jewellery, it was a ridiculous amount of gear.

He said "I'll catch you later." And that's how it went and I gathered everything remaining up, and I mean everything, and bagged it. I put what bags I could into the furnace, the balance I actually furnaced at a place at Mitcham, and some of it went to a furnishing factory in White City.

If the Great Train Robbers had done such a thorough job and burned everything at Leatherslade Farm, they would never have been caught, because that's what got them all nicked. The lawyer who was arranging their clean-out of the slaughter didn't do his bit.

The police never knew, in actual fact, where the slaughter was, so there was no way the Police could turn up there and look for clues.

Johnny took the van away from Kennington because he had a lot more to move, being his share plus all the tom, plus money for other members of the gang who were not at the slaughter. I was going to move the van as we had planned, but he said "leave it, I'll move it." He was fairly confident that the Old Bill would not have a description of the van, but there still was an element of risk that someone might have spotted the van and tied it in with our brilliant night's work. Besides, I wasn't wearing turtles, gloves. No point in leaving any dabs if you don't have to. The van wasn't nicked, but had been bought specially for the job.

When the cars were finished with they were dumped in the grounds of a notorious block of flats nearby, with their windows wide open. They probably got stripped, very rapidly. They would have ended up in short order with no wheels, and eventually on the dump, courtesy of the local council. What we normally used to do with any car or van used for work, was to take it out to a place like Scratchwood and leave it with the doors unlocked and windows open. The dew soon gets rid of the finger prints. Bits used to disappear off these motors, till they looked just like the victims of joy riders.

When I had given everything a good wipe I locked up, and after dumping one of the cars in a nearby estate, left for home in the cold morning light. I hadn't felt better in long time. I didn't sleep till the next night: it felt good.

Johnny had bought all the gear from the other blokes who were really only too pleased to be going home with a cash only swag. Johnny didn't say precisely where he drove to, but south to nearby Glanville Road, Brixton, or south-west to Norwood would have been a good bet. A greengrocer friend of Johnny's, who lived a short distance south of the slaughter in Norwood was later convicted of using his premises for a share out of money and jewellery from the raid.

The police thought that the jewellery had been taken to the continent for fencing, but I don't think it went further that night than south London. Later next day Johnny was again seen deep in conversation with Dave Ranger in the Circle Club.

Johnny certainly did not get home very early. When he did get home just before lunch, he was muddy, tired and ready for a hot bath and a kip. His wife Vivienne instead gave him a mouthful. "How dare you stay out all night." It didn't matter if he had been working, he must have been with another woman after, why else had he come home so late. She demanded to know exactly what he had been up to. Johnny had been through all this before, and wasn't going to be baited into telling her what in fact he had been up to. She knew, but was not going to let it rest till he had told her in detail. He tried all the usual words, then finally slammed the bathroom door in her face.

She was much younger than him, by 18 years, at 33, not beautiful in the traditional sense, but sexy in a way that even strangers noticed. And she knew it, and she used it. She had been attracted to Johnny's money, to his undoubted abilities as a keyman, to his status in the fraternity, and to his reserve which was quite different from her string of previous lovers, villains all. She had seduced him on their first date, he was hooked, and they married soon after. He was beginning to find all the questions, all the little games, just a bit tiring.

He washed and changed. She attacked him again, why didn't he finish the DIY round the house, why was he always fiddling with those stupid locks, why did she have to slave in that crappy little kitchen, while he spent his nights out doing god knows what.

He gave in, "OK love lets go down to Hendon and get that kitchen you always wanted." She smiled, the world was a sweet place again. He was going to regret that snap decision for some time to come.

Chapter 10 - Arrests & Grassing

The robbery took place on the night of Thursday 24th April 1975. The first report of the robbery appeared in a tiny two column inch report in the *Times* on Friday, the day after, where it was reported that "armed raiders escaped with about £300,000 in banknotes and an unknown amount of valuables." Neither the bank nor the police really knew how much was taken.

The next day the estimated figure rose to £249,000 in cash, partly in US dollars, plus nearly £1 million in jewellery. This figure was to continue growing till at the trial the figure of £2.5 million was mentioned. Later newspaper reports spoke of £8 million, and at the end of the trial by November 1976 of £10 million, but the true figure of £26 million was never publicly acknowledged.

Scotland Yard assumed that the jewellery would be fenced in Europe, so it rapidly notified Interpol. As a lot of the jewellery was large stones and very distinctive pieces, fencing them in England would have been difficult. Only one or two very major fences would have been able to handle this quality of tom. The exact contents of the deposit boxes remained unknown to the detectives, except where the owner was happy to come forward and supply a list of his property. In fact only 59 owners finally came forward, and not all of them wanted to give full details.

Not surprisingly, many box owners were not very forthcoming with details of what may well have been sensitive, undeclared or ill-gotten gains. In addition a large number of the owners were abroad, many of them being Americans keeping some of their assets offshore. They may not even have heard of the burglary till notified by the Bank.

One box owner who did come forward was Mrs. Farida Hall from

Indonesia, whose box was amongst the 89 opened, said it had contained gems worth £200,000, including nine distinctive rings, two brooches, two pendants and five pair of earrings, made in the almost pure 22 carat gold typical of Indian jewellery. She, like many other box holders, would not have had separate insurance on the contents of the box, presuming that the Bank was impregnable. Even allowing for some exaggeration by box owners hoping to claim against the Bank's insurance, this indication of average contents yields a rough figure when multiplied out of over £17 million.

Coin collectors and dealers also used the Bank's vaults, one of which feared he had lost coins worth at least six figures. Luise Rainer, the former actress, and wife of Robert Knittel (a director of William Collins the publishers), who had been banking at the Bank of America for 30 years, and who had had a box there for 15 years, lost many pieces of jewellery, some of them family heirlooms. Ms Rainer must have thought that her belongings were not safe anywhere, as a year earlier, whilst attending a wedding in Italy, she stopped in Milan for a few minutes to see the famous Duomo cathedral, and had £45,000 worth of jewellery stolen from her car. This might uncharitably be seen as carelessness, but with the Bank vault she could be forgiven for thinking that here her belongings were safe at last.

Some box owners waited years before claiming against the Bank. One, Eric Sosnow, 67, chairman of United City Merchants, and his wife Sylvia claimed to have lost jewellery worth nearly £1 million from just one box, but did not issue a writ against the Bank till June 1978.

Other boxes contained things for which their owners could not claim including guns and even a Mauser machine pistol. One box, according to the *Daily Telegraph* [October 1976] belonged to Lady Rose Delbray, the youngest daughter of the late ninth Earl of Hardwicke. She and a friend, an American called Herman Hine had planned to organise a cross-Atlantic drugs run. The money to finance this was kept in their box at the Bank of America.

The Mayfair Bank Job

With the money they bought a fast former Admiral's Cup contestant yacht in Suffolk. From there a mostly amateur crew took it to Marbella in Spain. There after several false starts and a run-in with the Spanish equivalent of the coastguard they planned to take it over to Morocco and stock up, where drugs were plentiful, cheap, and semi-legal. On the run across the Atlantic, the navigator and part-time chef, who was learning his trade from books on navigation as they went, managed to sail in ever increasing circles.

Finally one of the crew came down with a burst appendix, and in the process of getting help and attempting to land on the east coast of the States, got themselves arrested. They were not best pleased when they discovered that their box at the Bank of America had been one of those opened and ransacked by the robbers.

One of the detectives leading the investigation, Detective Chief Inspector Johnny Peel, said, "This was certainly not a matter of luck, it was a well-planned, professional job. We are up against a good team of professional thieves."

The senior Bank of America official in the UK at the time of the robbery was Bruce Mitchell, vice-president and manager of the Bank's City branch where Banner also worked as an electrician, was quoted as saying "I would classify any loss as too much... a loss we would prefer not to have." For him it was every bank manager's worst nightmare come true, and having to explain why it happened to his superiors in the US was a truly grueling task. After the first raid why hadn't they tightened up the security a bit more than just adding a new alarm? Several members of the Bank's staff were later laid off. The ripples of the robbery spread out and affected a larger number of lives than the participants ever dreamed.

Old Bill got to know it was an inside job. They got the twig it was inside job because keys and combination numbers were involved. Although the gang had drilled a few speculative holes in the doors to throw the police off the scent, a lock expect confirmed that the vault door was actually opened with the combination rather than via the drill holes and feeler keys.

When the Bank of America robbery was first discovered the police did an automatic security check, like they would anywhere, to see if it was an inside job. They grilled a number of staff, including the hapless computer staff, who were initially thought by the police to be implicated. They could not believe that the team of burglars could happily work away in the vault, whilst leaving three members of bank staff wandering around untouched for over an hour, unless of course these three were accomplices.

The police initially didn't know how it was done, but they knew somebody must have had the combination. So they sent for their records and they found Banner had form, a prison record. Because of the security that was in place, and the fact that two different people had the lock combinations, it was inconceivable that the job was done without inside help. The doors were simply opened using those combinations: someone had to be in with the gang.

They talked to every member of staff who could have been involved. Inevitably they came to Banner, who they by then realised had a criminal record for handling stolen goods. They followed Banner to see if he would meet up with members of the gang. Finally the police arrested Banner at 9.30 pm on Friday in the Kings Head pub in Roehampton High Street, SW15, the day after the raid. Detective Chief Inspector Peel pulled him in for questioning. They also called at his home in Battersea, where his mother answered the door. "What's Stewart done now?" was all she could say.

So they went to work on Banner. Now don't forget he couldn't disappear could he? First he has got a job to hold down. Secondly he's also going to get something like £100,000 for his eye in the ceiling job, his information, and for what he did. Several of the team, especially Willy suggested very forcibly that he take a little holiday, so that everyone could get their gear sorted out, before Old Bill came sniffing round and grilling Banner. But Banner thought it was better to pretend that nothing had happened. He assumed that it would go like the first job, and he didn't really expect a pull from the cozzers.

The same night the police searched his house. They took the place apart. Under a loose floorboard they found a bag containing lock dials and another bag containing a combination lock mechanism. Both had been given to him by Freddie Leaf and Johnny Wilde, in an effort to identify the types of locks current in the Bank of America. Unfortunately, Banner had taken his 'homework' home, instead of either returning it or ditching it. Perhaps he thought it would come in handy some other time, God knows why.

Banner was interviewed at West End Central police station, just off Regent Street in Saville Row. It was a long interview. The police knew they had hit pay dirt, and they were not about to let it get away from them. Banner started by denying any involvement, but faced with the practice locking mechanisms, and the apparent certainty of the police, he began to waver. It's part of the technique. The police make out either that they know exactly what had happened, or that someone else has grassed you up. If you are not wise to that trick, you more than likely spill the beans, when they were really only trying it on.

The clincher as far as the police were concerned was when he was told that the gang had used guns. The effect on Banner was noticeable.

He said that he would like to answer some of the questions, but would not make a written statement. The thin end of the wedge had been inserted. DCI Peel, who was a rather tall scholarly looking person, played the friendly cop, whilst another cozzer took the hard line, threatening Banner with a long term for armed robbery.

The police kept coming back to the guns and the violence of the armed robbery, exaggerating the events of that night for Banner's benefit. He hadn't heard how things really went from the team, so when the cozzer said it was an armed and violent robbery, Banner half believed him, and said about the guns, "honest, I didn't know a thing about them." That was too much, and Banner was soon well on his way, "I don't like violence. I was told in the first instance there was going to be eight involved, and no violence."

The police asked him again who had put him up to the job, and after a bit of pissing around, he decided that he didn't want to take the rap alone and dropped Jimmy O'Shaughnessy right in it. Banner should at least have observed the fraternity's 'three day rule': nobody says anything for at least three days to give their mates a chance to make a clean run for it. With Banner it was closer to three minutes than three days!

The cozzers had been observing Jimmy throughout Friday anyway. because of the earlier tip off. As Banner was being interviewed, Jimmy and his girlfriend Jane Spalding were driving through London in their green Range Rover, on their way to see a 'business' acquaintance about the disposal of Jimmy's share of the proceeds of the robbery. It was going to cost them about ten percent to move it into a safe bank account overseas, but it was worth it. After that, not a care.

They were feeling pretty good, both were bubbling with a subdued excitement. It had come off cleanly without a hitch. Jane, who had been worrying for the last few months, felt as if a large weight had been lifted for her, "Let's go and celebrate at Drakes in the Fulham Road tomorrow night, when all this money business has been fixed up," she chortled. She could even give up her job if she wanted to. Who needed champagne.

At quarter past ten on the same night as the police arrested Banner, the car following Jimmy and Jane was instructed to move in. Other cars were detailed to the area, and at twenty past there was a screech of brakes and the car following pulled in front of the Range Rover. Almost immediately other cars boxed in the Range Rover, and the door of Jimmy's car was being yanked open. The policeman who got the driver's side door open demanded to know his name. Jimmy, normally pretty cool, was stunned. The job had gone off as sweet as a nut: why was he now surrounded by cozzers? It wasn't right. He and Jane were arrested and cautioned. Both of them were taken to West End Central Police Station, where Banner was still being questioned.

The Mayfair Bank Job

DCI Peel came out of the interview room where he had been questioning Banner, and after lighting another cigarette, started the process of questioning O'Shaughnessy. At first Jimmy denied everything, knowing that in almost every case the police tactic is to pretend they know much more than they really do, and a cool 'no comment' or a straight denial was the best way to prevent then learning anything more. Jimmy had learnt long ago that fencing with the cozzers was not a useful exercise. Sooner or later you let out just a few more pieces of information than you intend to: it's better that a 'no comment' makes you look guilty, than an accidental remarks gives then the clue to prove that you are guilty.

Jimmy's alibi was that he had been at his mother's place. He knew she would back him up come hell or high water. Unlike Banner's parents, who wanted him to 'make a clean break," Mrs. O'Shaughnessy could be relied upon to back up whatever he son said. The police drove the Range Rover to the car park under the nick, while Jimmy and Jane stayed overnight in the not too uncomfortable cells at West End Central.

By the next day, the Saturday 26th April, Banner had been convinced that he should sing. He admitted he was involved, and after a bit of verbal fencing described what he had seen as a harmless burglary to the police. He volunteered, "I'll do my bird, but I want everyone to know I had nothing to do with shooters."

Banner had several visits from his worried mother and father who encouraged him to 'tell the truth' and make a clean breast of it. He justified his grassing by telling the police, "It's only because they used guns that I'm telling you all this. I don't want none of that. This should have been the sweetest job ever...." Indeed so it should have been.

Nobody except Freddie knew he was going to be carrying a gun. In addition several of the team members had picked up the machine pistols they had found in the boxes and were waving them around on the night of the robbery, more as a lark than anything else. The police emphasised the darker side of this to the already very scared Banner.

Banner wrote and signed a short statement to the effect that he had given Freddie Leaf and Jimmy O'Shaughnessy information about the Bank's security systems, but that didn't know anything about the robbery. He had already verbally 'lollied' O'Shaughnessy, although he did not know the whole gang. But not everybody got grassed, and some that did, didn't get arrested. Freddie Leaf for example had left for Marbella in Spain, and was later traced to Morocco, Germany, Greece and eventually Austria. Although he was only directly involved in the first raid of October 1974, the police were still very keen to feel his collar. When in the following year they discovered him in Spain, they immediately applied for extradition, but that's another story that we may get to later.

Banner's statement was first taken round by DCI Peel to O'Shaughnessy's cell so that Jimmy could see where he stood. Banner had effectively tried to get himself off the hook as a co-conspirator, and put the whole job down to Jimmy and Freddie Leaf. Well Freddie was well away, and he was left to face the music.

Jimmy kept denying everything, while he was trying to suss out what the cozzers actually knew. He was keen not to involve Jane, who although she had been present at one or two of his early discussions with Freddie, was not really 'in on it.' Four hours later he knew the game was up, the police had found £75,000 of his stash, and there was no way he could deny it came from the Bank of America.

If the police had just busted him ten minutes later Jimmy would have been able to complete his arrangements, and all his money would have been on its way, and safe. As it was, the cozzers systematically raided every place that Jimmy had visited in the previous 24 hours, and found £75,000 which he had set on one side for his immediate expenses.

He had left this in his old flat in Beech court, Harroby Street, W1, just off the Edgeware Road, "just in case," when he had stopped off at on his way from the Bank to the slaughter on the night of the robbery. He hoped that nobody would think to look there. He had stowed it in the back of an old cupboard in a suitcase. He had kept on his old flat when he bought the much larger house in Manorgate Road, Kingston-upon-Thames a year or so before the robbery.

The police were not in any mood to let up: almost unlimited overtime had been sanctioned, and they were getting results, the sort of results most cozzers can only dream about. The Commissioner himself was being pressured from very high up to get results. This was not just a small foreign bank that had been done over for a few hundred thousand pounds, this was much bigger. How big could only be judged by the sudden burst in telex and radio traffic between the American Embassy and Langley in the States, home of the CIA.

When the police accurately described to Jimmy his case containing the money, and admitted that they had to break off the combination locks, Jimmy knew that he was done up like a kipper. He figured that the only deal he could hope to do was to co-operate with them in the hope of a lighter sentence.

"What's the position if I tell you the part I played, just the part I played? You've got my money back, my share, and as far as I was concerned, there was no violence. I've gained nothing out of the robbery now."

Of course £75,000 was his 'just in case' money: he had no intention of telling the cozzers where his real stash was hidden.

"If I agree to make a statement, would you let my wife go because she's got nothing at all to do with all this?" he volunteered.

DCI Peel, who was interviewing him said, "No promises mind you, but I guess we can do something, if you make it easier for all of us."

"Very well then, I will go down on paper that I was the organiser, and actually took part on the night, and all that." When DCI Peel had got the basics on paper, he went off to find his superior, none other than the tall graying head of the Flying Squad, Chief Superintendent Jack Slipper, famous for his pursuit of that other robber Ronnie Biggs. Slipper seemed to have a 'thing' about catching the robbers involved in the really big hauls.

You should have seen their faces when Slipper strode into the room, keen to see the latest of the Bank of America robbers, all sorted out and ready to confess. Instead he saw one of his golfing partners from the posh Sudbrook Park Golf Club, near Kingston, where both Jimmy and he played.

"Christ, Jimmy, what are you doing here." It took Slipper a split second to realise the boob he had made, and quickly turned his greeting into a more frosty business like tone. It did not do to let his officers see that he was on first name terms with major villains.

That same day, after giving the police the details of how the jobs had been planned, Banner asked if he could speak to DCI Peel privately. Maybe he wanted a deal, maybe he even thought he could get off scot-free. He said he wanted to assist in the recovery of the proceeds of the robbery as far as he was able, at least in relation to his own share. He admitted to DCI Peel that somebody else was holding the money and jewellery for him, but he did not want to incriminate that person.

Whatever promises were made by DCI Peel, they were not kept, for Banner's minder eventually got 2 years for his efforts. Anyway at this point Banner was reassured, and he set off with them in a police car to Byfleet in Surrey.

They stopped at a phone box, and the police allowed Banner to make a private telephone call. He called his mate Eddie 'Tag' Garthwaite and arranged to meet him at the Marquis of Granby pub on the bypass. At 8.00 pm his mate arrived and Banner said, "Look Tag, I'm nicked. This is the law. Give them the money."

Garthwaite, who had only just finished hiding the money for Banner the previous evening, was both terrified and pissed off, terrified that he might be implicated in what the police were still calling an armed robbery, and pissed off that his sizeable slice of the action which he had conned out of the easy going Banner was about to evaporate.

Garthwaite agreed, and they all got back into the car to make the journey to the cottage deep in Kent where Garthwaite had arranged the burial of the loot. Arriving just before midnight, the police followed Garthwaite's directions to Brenchley and the home of a civil servant aged 27. This individuual, who lived on the edge of Palmers Green, demanded to know what the fuss was about. When Garthwaite introduced Banner and DCI Peel he quietened down. Protesting that he had only been doing a friend a favour he helped find the police shovels, and pointed out a newly turned piece of earth in the adjoining forest, located just six paces from an old beech tree.

About 3 feet down they found a plastic Osma pipe that had been professionally sealed at both ends. Inside were plastic bags packed with great care. In the bags was part of Banner's cash share of the proceeds and a number of pieces of jewellery, amounting to some £68,000.

Later Garthwaite was charged with dishonestly receiving from Banner £32,810 plus US$25,400 and some 32 items of jewellery, one item worth about £10,000.

As Banner was originally scheduled to receive a one-eighth whack on the first abortive raid, it is possible that he received that amount on the second successful raid. He certainly received at least £100,000. What is certain though is that only £68,000 was recovered.

Chapter 11 - Arrests & Escapes

The police did not have to entirely rely upon Stewart Banner's grassing. In fact if the police had not been tipped off several weeks before that a big bank job was about to be pulled, they would not have been able to pounce quite so rapidly, because they had been closely watching major 'faces' in the London bank robbing fraternity, which included several members of the actual team who were on the job.

The source of this tip off was never made public, but in retrospect it seem likely to have been the wife of one on the main team members, who when she was arrested was first charged under a false name, and who later made a career out of grassing up her friends and lovers. A second possibility was Mickey Jevons, one of the team members who only received a very light one and a half year sentence, although there seems to be little reason for him to have grassed before the event. Mickey however was later turned by a detective called Tony Lundy, and did grass on his mates in another job. A third possibility was Johnny O'Connell who was only involved in the planning of the first raid, and who for his pains and potential for grassing was later shot in the legs with a sawn-off shotgun. He may have been less than happy about the second raid.

However when Johnny thought back over the events leading up to the second robbery, he remembered that the potential fence he had spoken to, Dave Ranger, also had close contacts with some well-connected policemen from Scotland Yard, including the infamous Lundy. For a long time he pondered on this. However we are jumping ahead of events.

For several weeks the police had been secretly watching various members of the firm, as well as a range of other 'faces' involved in major league robbery business. Meetings had been observed and comings and goings noted. After the raid, the initial police response was to pull in people all over the place and see if anyone cracked or talked. Some of the team had had the cozzers on their tails throughout the Friday and Saturday after the raid, so that when they were finally arrested on Saturday night, the police had a fairly good idea of where they had been and who they had met with. It really is surprising that given this intense surveillance, that the police did not recover more of the gear. The crucial hours immediately after the raid, was sufficient for most of the team to hide the majority of their proceeds.

As a result of this tip-off, and their accumulated observations, four men and five women were almost immediately arrested on or before the night of Saturday 26th April, just two days after the robbery. Everyone concerned was surprised at the speed of the police response, and some of the team had not yet properly secured their stashes. The same night along with these arrests approximately £140,000 and a bag of jewellery was recovered.

For Scotland Yard it was something of a triumph. Detective Superintendent Bob Robinson had welded together teams of detectives from West End Central, led by Detective Chief Inspector Johnny Peel and Flying Squad men headed by Detective Chief Inspector Michael O'Leary, without encountering too much of the usual inter-force rivalries. Even the undercover squad C11, were putting systematic pressure on their usual contacts in the underworld, listening out for a whisper, even a casual reference to 'the big one.'

This team however had more than its fair share of lucky breaks. Without Banner's testimony and the tip-off, it might have been a much harder graft to come up with any answers. The robbery itself had left precious few clues, and the cars used were not sighted by any witnesses, except Willy's parking indiscretion.

One of the first arrests was Johnny Wilde at his home in Palmers Green. He was surprised to see them, but remained calm in the knowledge that his stash was well and truly secure, and he had two firm alibis for the night in question. What did he have to worry about? After all if they tried him, and he was found not guilty, he could never be tried again for the same crime — much better to have done and get it over with. He even welcomed the idea. He was not getting any younger, and it would be nice to put the trial behind him so he could simply get on with enjoying his life. What was a few months on remand compared to a lifetime of ease.

He certainly had not told his volatile wife Viv where he had hidden the tom, or what he had done with the huge pile of currency. He could not trust her to hold her tongue, and already he regretted that she knew that 'something big' was due to go off, some weeks before the robbery actually happened. With Viv however it was a totally different reaction, she turned on the police with, "What the fuck do you lot want. Just leave my husband alone. He ain't done nothing."

They cautioned Johnny, trying to ignore Viv who kept screaming abuse and plucking at their sleeves. If she was trying to play the distraught wife, if she was trying to convince Johnny, then maybe she overplayed her hand. He left with them, thankful of the relative peace of the squad car.

On Sunday 27th April after a night of arrests, running round the home counties and digging in dark woods the police were back questioning Banner.

Forensic experts were immediately put to work examining Banner's recovered money and jewels, whilst a team of detectives worked round the clock to collate the loss reports by the Bank's 89 customers who had had their boxes rifled, trying desperately to circulate a list around jewelers and dealers before either the jewellery was sold or was fenced.

Johnny however was far too canny to fence the stuff he had acquired till the first rush of interest died down. In fact much of his stash was to wait till 1991 before it again saw the light of day.

On Monday the 28th April, the number of people being questioned had grown from four to nine men plus two women, the women being Johnny's wife and Jimmy's girlfriend Jane. Jane was finally released on Tuesday 29th April, on bail.

She worked as the private secretary of the Ambassador of one of the Scandinavian Embassies, and had missed work on Monday.

As soon as she was released she phoned the Ambassador, and asked to see him on a personal matter. She and Jimmy had in the past looked after the Ambassador's dog and were on fairly friendly terms with him. She went round to see him at the residence in Park Street. Because she knew that he would hear sooner or later, Jane outlined more or less exactly what had happened to the Ambassador, and offered her resignation.

As she had expected, he refused to accept it, "I'm extremely sorry, my dear, to hear what a predicament you and Jimmy have got yourself into, but I wouldn't hear of accepting your resignation at a time like this. As far as I am concerned this does not affect your job."

Jane almost broke down with relief at his kind words, but unfortunately, the pressure being applied from the top, caused the Foreign Office to eventually persuade the Ambassador that he could not retain a secretary whose boyfriend had been involved in a major crime.

For the next couple of days the police intensively grilled the suspects till on Wednesday 30th April, just six days after the robbery, seven of the suspects were formally remanded at Great Marlborough Street Magistrates court. The men were all taken to Brixton Prison to await trial.

What had taken 9 months planning, and had been executed almost without a hitch, fell apart in such a short time. Unlike Leaf who thought that changing countries was the best way to put distance between yourself and the law, most of the firm had deep roots in London. Like the Great Train Robbers before then, they would have felt uncomfortable living in a foreign country, unlike the wave of criminals who comfortably settled into the lifestyle of southern

Spain in the 1980s. They liked their regular drinking haunts, their wives and families, and a good cuppa tea, and had no intention of leaving the UK.

As it happens, Banner was the weakest link in the chain, with a few of the others not exactly adhering to the criminal code of no grassing. The police used to the greatest advantage the natural distrust felt by many members of the fraternity for their colleagues from 'foreign' parts of London. On the other hand, most of the main team members gave back very little if any of the huge amounts they had got away with, and were determined to plead not guilty.

Those members of the firm who were remanded on 30 April, 1975 at the Great Marlborough Magistrates' court included Stewart Banner (who had lead the police to the others), Jimmy O'Shaughnessy (who had done much of the planning), and Johnny Wilde.

Banner had been directly involved with both O'Shaughnessy and knew Johnny Wilde from having helped him reconnoiter the Bank's premises after dark. The three were charged with robbery and conspiracy to rob.

With them were also charged some of their friends and accomplices who had helped to hide or move their stashes.

The police treated these friends as receivers, and knew that they were not directly involved in the robbery. The first one arrested was Edward Arthur Garthwaite, aged 33, a croupier of Green Lane Close, Byfleet, Surrey, who had been Banner's accomplice in secreting his share of the proceeds. Garthwaite was charged with dishonestly receiving, to which after speaking to Banner he pleaded guilty. Despite police reassurances, he finally received a 2 year sentence.

Apart from helping Banner with his share of the robbery, Garthwaite may also have tried to fence some of the Krugerrands on his own account. Alternatively, he may simply have had his fingers in a number of pies. On 7th July in the same year he was also committed for trial at the Central Criminal court (the Old Bailey) from Marlborough Street Magistrates' court, charged with obtaining gold Krugerrands and cash worth altogether £18,552 by deception and various other offences. It seems likely that the Krugerrands may well have been part of the haul from the Bank of America job. His co-defendant was a Lebanese Arab called Abdul al Hassan, aged 24, who lived in Brouncker Road Acton, London, W3. Although Hassan was not apparently caught up in the Bank of America robbery, he was bailed for £15,000 whilst Garthwaite was bailed for only £100. He had obviously fallen on hard times, or the police were very sure he was not going to make a run for it.

Garthwaite's friend who helped hide Banner's share in a wood near Brenchley, Essex, was later discharged.

Garthwaite also had an address in Camden Road, London NW1, just as did one of the women also charged in the Bank of America trial, a 'Miss Valerie Stitcher-Stewart.' This was almost certainly a cover name for Vivienne Wilde, Johnny's wife, who was later tried under her own name. She was charged by the police with dishonestly receiving 19 £20 notes, what was left of some of the money given to her by Johnny.

Another caught up in the aftermath of the robbery was Jeffrey Edmond Stitcher, 37, another greengrocer like Johnny Wilde. He lived in Elder Road, West Norwood, London, SE27, interestingly a short trip just south of the location of the slaughter. Stitcher was also charged with dishonestly receiving.

Jeffrey Houdan, was however a very different kettle of fish. He was 50, a decorator (like Freddie Leaf) of Glanville Road Brixton, London SW2. This was no more than a five minute drive south of the slaughter, and ironically just across a sports field from Brixton jail. At the time of his arrest he gave his address as "of no fixed abode," covering up his real address for as long as possible from the police, perhaps to give someone time to clear up his place. Jeffrey was only charged with dishonest receiving. To this he pleaded guilty, but as we shall see he drew a much longer prison sentence than the other hangers-on and fences. He received 12 years instead of the more typical 2 to 3 for receiving. Although he handed back £32,000 of the stolen money, it seems likely from the length of his sentence that he may well have known more about the final location of some of the loot than he was prepared to say.

On Saturday 3rd May, Willy Gavroche was arrested and charged with conspiracy, a charge later changed to robbery. On the same day the others were again remanded in custody. Willy however had really dropped himself in it. As we have seen, he parked his own car, a red Ford, in Bruton Street, Mayfair, near the Bank, just after midday on the day of the robbery, hoping to put enough in the meter to tide it over till 4 pm. With luck he thought the parking wardens will not spot it till 6.30 pm when the parking restrictions came off. For Willy this was a big mistake — he would not normally take his own car on a job — he must have been feeling supremely confident.

However a traffic warden spotted and ticketed Willy's car. Willy didn't know about it till he retrieved his car in the small hours of the next morning, but by then the damage had been done. He paid his fine soon afterwards hoping that nobody would notice, but the police scanned the parking ticket database for that day and the previous couple of weeks, matching the plate numbers against those of known robbers, and of course they hit pay dirt with Willy's car. Willy had sensibly gone on holiday for a week immediately after the raid. However as soon as he returned home on the 3rd of May, the police arrested him.

After singing for several weeks, Banner was finally persuaded to make a written statement on 16th May. By now he was too far in to go back. It took him till 29th of May to finish dictating his statement.

It was not till 21 May that Harold Scott, 42, was pulled in by the police for questioning about conspiring to rob the Bank. He gave his profession as a company director, and he came from the East End of London, old Kray brothers territory in Mansford Street, Bethnal Green. Seven weeks later he was discharged at

Marlborough Magistrates court, but it is interesting to speculate that he was possibly the East End 'representative.'

At the same hearing, Johnny Mason, aged 44, who was arrested about the same time, was also charged with conspiring to rob the bank, and bailed for the relatively small sum of £20,000. He was one of the 'Famous Five' henchmen of the Kray twins, and obviously was another East End input into the job. He too was later to be acquitted for lack of evidence.

Also by this hearing, Mickey Jevons had been picked up and charged with conspiring to rob the bank, and bailed for, the relatively small sum of £20,000. Here the police had a much stronger case, but Jevons who had considerable skill in handling the police, although found later guilty, only drew the smallest sentence of all the firm, a mere 18 months. Given Mickey Jevons's cleverness, it is not impossible that he did a deal with the police.

Paul Caldwell had heard what had happened to the others and managed to stay ahead of the police for several weeks after the robbery. He thought about leaving the country, but dismissed the idea. He was a difficult man to trace.

Although he lived just near Johnny Wilde, as soon as he heard about the others arrests, he became very wary about where he went and who he was seen with. He curbed his lifestyle, but after a few weeks of avoiding the cozzers, he began to relax his guard. He was reported as having been seen dining out at a good restaurant, and the police who felt he was deliberately thumbing his nose at them decided to hot up their investigations.

He had a number of narrow escapes, and on one occasion he stopped at traffic lights in his well-known blue Mercedes, and a Flying Squad car pulled up alongside of him. Paul could not resist turning and smiling. The sergeant recognised him from his picture that had been well circulated, and dived out of his car and made a grab at the door handle of the Mercedes. Paul ignored the red light and stepped on it leaving him sprawling on the ground. By the time the police had collected themselves he had made several tight turns and disappeared into the traffic.

He was sighted on two further occasions. A man with a weak stomach might have been tempted to assume a disguise or even leave the country: not Paul. He even tried to keep up with his regular girlfriends. One particular girlfriend he used to ring from call boxes had her phone tapped by the cozzers. Unfortunately for him, Paul tended to use call boxes in the same area, so the police covered all the public phone boxes in the area with squad cars. When he next called her, they traced the call while the squad cars pounced on all the phone boxes in the area currently in use. That's how much they wanted him. In one of the boxes the found Paul.

He was finally arrested by Sergeant Willis of the Flying Squad on 30 June 1975. When he was cautioned he replied, "Don't give me that load of old bollocks, Sergeant. There's a couple of grand in it for you, if I can make just one phone call!" He was trying to make the call which would have secured his stash of money, and at the same time provided enough cash for him to hire the best Brief around. Sergeant Willis agreed to the deal if Paul would make the call in front of him. When for obvious reasons he refused Willis's offer he was taken to West End Central Police Station, which was being used to co-ordinate the investigations into the robbery, and banged up.

He had just finished putting the last touches on the new extension to his house in Southgate, London, N14, just a short walk from Johnny Wilde's home in the adjoining postcode of N13. Paul had stowed his share of the proceeds safely and was looking forward to a comfortable life. He had not seriously thought about leaving the country.

That however was not the end for Caldwell, who could see that if he could just give the police the slip, his newly acquired wealth would enable him to start a new life even in the UK. Before the officers were able to start questioning him he asked if he could go to the toilet to clean up. After peeing he covered his face and hands with a lot of water. Pretending not to be able to see he began waving rounds his arms, "Say, mate give us a towel will ya, I can't see a damn thing." The officer crossed the washroom to get some paper towels for him, just as he brushed the water from his eyes with his sleeve, and made flying leap through the door to the toilets, and bounded downstairs.

Not used to that kind of audacity, two officers actually stepped backwards to get out of his way. He reached the reception area in a few seconds, and dashed through a group of startled officers. The door was locked. He made a split second decision and launched himself at a small half open window. He was just scrambling through when the knot of policemen gathered their scattered wits and made a concerted rush for Paul's fast disappearing legs. Even with all those hands grabbing at him, Paul had the presence of mind to undo his trousers, hoping to still escape even without his trousers. By this time reinforcements had arrived and he was hauled by his ankles back through the window. He made several other bids for freedom, and in the end he was handcuffed even when surrounded by 10 or 15 policemen on his way two and from court.

Apart from Freddie Maiser and a rumoured two other minor lookout members of the team, the cozzers had picked up all the faces that were known to Banner, and a few more besides. Two of those still on the loose at the time of the trial, were seem wining and dining it a not inexpensive Chelsea restaurant.

Every one of the team had their own specialities, and Jimmy O'Shaughnessy, who had masterminded the whole operation had one or two specialities of his own which the police had not bargained for...

Chapter 12 - O'Shaughnessy Escapes & Banner's Trial

Those of the team who were remanded in custody were obliged, because of the way the law is, to go to Great Marlborough Street Magistrates' court once a week to be repeatedly remanded, until the trial. It was the law that they had to be formally remanded every seven days, rather than being held indefinitely at the pleasure of the court. Although there was no question that any of them would be granted bail, this farce had to be endured every week.

Every Monday the accused were remanded they had to go through the procedure of being handed back their clothes and private property, handed over by the prison authorities to the police who would take then by prison van with police escorts to Great Marlborough Magistrates' court where they would apply for bail, be refused, and get remanded in custody for yet another week. They would then be put back in the prison van and be driven back to Brixton Prison, where they would give up their private property and be locked up again. Each man was locked in a separate cell opening off from a central corridor which ran from the back doors to the front of the van. The cells were cold, and had a hard bench seat, so cramped that each man's knees were forced hard against the steel wall in front of him. The windows were barred, small and high up, and the van was more like a cattle truck than a coach. In winter the heating never worked properly so they were freezing cold. In summer they could be boiling hot. At least each man was left alone with his own thoughts for the duration of the journey. Being remand prisoners they were treated marginally better than those who had already been convicted.

Jimmy spent this time thinking, and decided that escape was the only answer. It seemed likely that he was going down for a long sentence, and escaping might well solve all his problems. The feeling of being herded like cattle was repeated as the van docked at the court: the van's doors did not open till the great iron gates closed, and they were herded down into the cells with sometimes as many as 15 policemen in the yard watching.

Jimmy decided that the chances of escaping from Brixton were close to nil, and that the van was almost as secure without outside help, so it had to be the court. The weeks went by, and he started to become very familiar with the routine. Perhaps the best chance lay with the jostling mixture of solicitors, clerks, accused and policemen, as they moved down the crowded corridors of the court building, "it was all a bit of a crush most days."

At the hearing at the Great Marlborough Street Magistrates' court, on 28th July 1975, as the accused were on their way from the courts back to the cells, O'Shaughnessy made his move.

There was a door off the passage down which the prisoners were taken which led to the bail room, where those who had made bail were allowed to pass to the outside world after they had satisfied the bail requirement. Jimmy noticed that solicitors and clerks seemed to have great freedom of movement to and from that room, so on this day he made sure that his civvy clothes were totally up to scratch. During the hearing he asked his solicitor if he could have a look at the bundle of depositions bound with the usual pink legal ribbon, a carry over from Dickensian days, which had been brought to the trial. Clutching these and striding along purposefully he looked more like a solicitor's clerk than one of the accused.

As he went down the corridor past a small toilet he dived into it. When his bunch had passed he went back along the corridor and dived into the barristers' robbing room, but nobody sees him. He put on a barrister's robe and just walked purposefully into the bail room, carrying his brief with him. The policeman guarding the door opened it in response to his very assured, 'thank you very much indeed." Holding his breath he walked across the bail room and using the same approach on the outer door, and got it opened for him by the police guard.

Can you imagine that? He just walked out the court! Some of his co-defendants say that he must have had help, that maybe he bought his way out with money or information. Whatever happened, he needed style and a cool head to pull it off.

He reached the street and made his way down Carnaby Street, turned into Beak Street and called a cab. He was free. Of course when you are on remand and you go to court you only have on you what you were arrested with. Anyway, he's away in a cab and goes to ground.

At the time a lot of people were saying that it was set up for him to do that. Jimmy was very resourceful, but it seemed highly unlikely that he could have escaped just by brazening it out, but that's how that situation went. It smelt to high heaven to the rest of the team still on remand in Brixton. How did he get away with it without help?

For those on remand, August and September passed very slowly. On 22nd September, 1975 Stewart Banner was tried at the Old Bailey, or the Central Criminal court as it is now called. He was arraigned on four counts.

The first charge was that in the course of the first raid, he had "entered as a trespasser... with intent to steal therein a quantity of money, and the contents of certain deposit boxes." He pleaded guilty, as indeed he had already agreed with the police and the CPS.

The second count was one of conspiracy, between January and March 1975, to rob the Bank of America branch at Walbrook in the City of London. Between the first and second raids, he had at Freddie Leaf's suggestion taken Johnny into this other branch to suss out if perhaps it would be an even easier target for robbery than the Mayfair branch. In the end they decided not to hit the Walbrook branch.

Nevertheless Banner pleaded guilty to this conspiracy charge, so as to get it off his chest.

The third charge laid against him was a technical and specific charge that he robbed the three computer staff of £143,245 in sterling, plus US$235,352, plus a quantity of travelers cheques, money orders and the contents of safe deposit boxes. Although the robbery was in fact against the Bank the charge was framed as if he had robbed the three staff of the Bank. The amounts of money were simply the amounts that the Bank could definitely prove ownership of. With the boxes the Bank could not definitely swear in court to the exact amount lost. Obviously as Banner was not there, this technical charge was denied: he pleaded not guilty, and the charge was set aside.

The fourth charge, was that he entered the premises of the Bank of America as a trespasser and there stole the amounts mentioned in the previous paragraph. The charge was framed as a burglary charge rather than a robbery. He pleaded guilty to this one.

Having got the pleas over, and having had them accepted by the court, the barrister for the prosecution, the flamboyant and portly Mr. Michael Corkery (assisted by Stephen Mitchell) proceeded to outline the history of the first break into the Mayfair branch. He explained that although the team had got into the bank, the drills had broken when the attempted to drill the vault door.

He went on to explain to the Judge the planning involved in casing the Walbrook branch. For a while Freddie thought that this branch was going to be easier, and Johnny had fixed up a set of keys for the team.

Finally the barrister got to second and successful break into the Mayfair branch of the Bank of America on 24th April that year. Judge King-Hamilton, QC, who was to go on to judge the rest of the defendants at a later date, expressed great surprise that Banner was able to wander in and out with Johnny Wilde and other accomplices without being queried by security. He felt it all sounded like a story from a *Boy's Own Annual*.

Banner described how on the very first trip, Johnny Wilde saw that the alarms were old and said that they should not give much trouble. He described to the court how he and Johnny had rifled through the manager's desk, going through his papers and finally his desk diary to see if there was any clue to the combination. It was typical behaviour for people to write down security passwords or lock combinations as clear as day in their diary or wallet, in the mistaken belief that nobody else is ever going to look there. They drew a blank, but did 'borrow' one set of keys they found in the drawer of the desk. Johnny copied the security key, using his tin of wax. Banner confirmed that that Johnny had in fact returned another evening to get precise measurements with his gauge. And so the trial proceeded with the presentation of such details to the Judge by the prosecuting barrister.

Explaining why he had decided to turn Queen's evidence, apart from the obvious reason that the cozzers had him bang to rights, Banner said, "I heard about the guns. Honest, I didn't know a thing about them. That was too much. I don't like violence. I was told, in the first instance, that there were going to be eight involved, and no violence. It is only because they used guns that I am telling you all this. I don't want none of that. This should have been the sweetest job ever."

To give Banner his due, all of his previous jobs had not involved violence, and relied upon stealth or deception. The Judge accepted Banner's statement that he thought it was going to be a simple burglary, and therefore that was the correct charge, rather than robbery.

When he had finished the Clerk of the court asked Banner if he wanted to have a further thirteen other unrelated offences, mainly of burglary and deception, taken into account. The list included aggravated burglary, obtaining property by deception, and conspiracy to commit burglary. Banner agreed as he had decided to make a clean breast of it, so that these offences did not catch up with him at a later date. Many of these were burglary and deception charges, involving his old mate and the original mastermind of the Bank of America job, Freddie Leaf.

In almost every case Banner took most of the risks, and Leaf took most of the money. Banner either was, or contrived to look as if he was the patsy in each of these jobs. He had fallen out with Leaf, and his information gave the police more of an incentive to find Leaf. Strangely, whilst giving his evidence Banner stated that Freddie Leaf had been present on the second raid at Mayfair, despite the fact that he was reputed to be overseas at the time. This was later to prove useful to Freddie, as a piece of Banner's evidence that could definitely be proven to be untrue.

On the first raid, Banner originally claimed to be in for a one eighth share of the proceeds. Probably from the second raid he only received a drink of about £100,000 for his information on the Bank and its security. Again Banner seems to have been the patsy, and not got his full whack, although later he only returned £68,000 of it.

Under cross-examination Detective Superintendent Robert Robinson described Banner as "a genius who had used his electronic talents for criminal purposes, pitting his wits against the most difficult problems and working out a solution." Perhaps, considering the number of 'experts' that Banner had taken into the Bank to solve specific problems, rather more glowing praise than Banner deserved. DS Robinson went even further and stated that Banner had been "used by ruthless big-time criminals." Poor Banner. That's not quite the way it was: Banner might have been encouraged by Freddie Leaf, but he was quite happy to put up this piece of work.

After going into his character and background, Banner's defense barrister Mr. Stephen Myerson put the big question to DS Robinson, "How would you rate him as a prospective witness for the prosecution in the case against others?"

This is the beginning of the trade off, a light sentence for a lot of lollying. Judge King-Hamilton appears to deliberately miss the point, "I do not understand the question."

Banner's barrister then attempts to put the point a little more clearly, "I am sorry. I am not making myself clear. To what extent is he necessary as a witness against prospective defendants in the

Bank of America case?", and with a touch of sarcasm, "I am sorry your Lordship did not understand."

Now this is the queue for the policeman to jump in and praise Banner's talent as a key prosecution witness, so that the barrister, Myerson, can come back with a carefully worded leniency plea. This is what Banner was pinning his hopes on.

Instead DS Robinson limply answers, "He, in the interests of justice, is a considerable witness, sir." The Judge, now aware of what is required leans over to help the policeman spit it out, "How do you rate him? He could be a good witness, not quite so good..."

DS Robinson comes back with a very noncommittal, "in my opinion, yes, sir." And so Banner, upon whom the prosecution case depended, is condemned with faint praise. The embarrassment evident in this very strained exchange is reflected in the actual court transcript, which for some reason has been retyped on this page only. Neither the police nor the judiciary felt very comfortable with this 'arrangement.'

The emphasis on professional criminals grassing members of their own gang was relatively new. Certainly the police had always had informers, but never on the 'supergrass' scale which was pioneered in the mid-seventies by DS Tony Lundy. It started with Lundy's first supergrass Ronnie Clare, and then the much more infamous Bertie Smalls the well-known bank robber, who was responsible for the conviction of numerous of his fellow members of the fraternity. In this case Banner provided enough evidence to convict the rest of the team, and hoped to get a very much reduced sentence.

The Judge sums up with one of the most pompous speeches about crime and punishment ever recorded, and awards Banner seven years for his trouble.

In the light of his sentence, it is surprising that he did not even hold his tongue for a few days, but blabbed almost as soon as he was arrested. He must have known that the police would pick him up as a matter of course. How is it possible that with his record he had not thought this through before allowing himself to get involved? It can't simply have been the use of a gun, as no one got hurt, indeed the computer staff were treated very decently. The only other possible motivation, is that Banner wanted to clear all the priors which he asked to be taken into consideration, so that he could start life with a clean slate, and perhaps with some of the proceeds. Possibly the police mislead him with promises of only a year or two, and he felt it was a worthwhile gamble.

In the end Banner got seven years, and was also marked for life as a grass: a heavy burden.

By Banner's trial some £300,000 had been recovered by the police, but there was still a lot more out there, so the police were more than slightly concerned that the money might finance either a break-out, as it had with the Great Train Robbers, or more subtly, the corruption of the jury in the forthcoming trial. It is after all only necessary to 'buy' two members of a jury to get an acquittal. The police needed Banner's statements, and they desperately needed to make sure that another member of the team would not make a fool of them as O'Shaughnessy had done.

Meanwhile other members of the firm, locked up in Brixton Prison, were making their preparations as best they could.

Chapter 13 - The Sweet Smell of Corruption

Because of Banner grassing, I had to find money for Johnny's defense. That wasn't awfully difficult, and Johnny was my mate. It was quite a cloak and dagger business though getting bits and pieces of jewellery fenced to get money together to pay briefs. Johnny wasn't on legal aid (is that a laugh), on a serious case you would really be stupid to use legal aid. If you're pleading guilty, you might use legal aid. But as far as they were concerned, he had got nothing except his greengrocer's shop. They don't know what you've really got and what you have not got, until you have been found guilty.

Now out of Johnny's share of the Bank of America haul there was a tiara. Johnny needed £80,000 anyway of which £40,000 was for a policeman who was going to do him a 'favour,' and £40,000 was for his Brief, Ronnie Trott at Hare Court. That's all I needed to know. So I went and got the tiara, which was handed over to me by a bloke called Tonka who was minding it for Johnny. Tonka is his Scottish nickname.

Why Tonka had to give it to me, I don't know, because as it happened I had to go back to his place eventually to sell it. Perhaps Johnny just wanted to be sure that the sale was conducted kosher. This tiara was worth retail about £325,000, and I had got to get £83,000 for it. That's not too bad is it, a quarter of its value? A fence will often only offer 10% of the value. My cut out of that was £3,000. Of the £80,000, the £40,000 for the solicitor was fairly straight forward, so I had simply to go and see him a couple of times to pay him out as the trial progressed. The equivalent of £40,000 at 1975 prices is considerably more today, that would keep him in 'refreshers' for a while.

The other £40,000 was not nearly so straightforward, it was meant

The Mayfair Bank Job

for a copper, a Detective Inspector 'Snead.' For obvious reasons, this is not his real name. He had previously asked Johnny for £500,000 in exchange for a promise to let him go, but Johnny reckoned that was beyond Snead's powers anyway. Johnny did however agree to give him £40,000 for a little something, and I had to meet this copper to arrange the payment. I arranged to meet him in a pub near the Old Vic theatre just south of the Thames.

I didn't know him, but he recognised me from my description: there has never been any trouble spotting me from my description. Anyway, I had to sit in the pub waiting for this geezer to come up and talk to me. The other cozzers called Snead 'the lawyer'; something to do with him being well up with all the wrinkles of the law. He knew all the angles, especially how to get out of trouble, he was as crooked as they go, you know, he had property in Spain and so on, even then, long before everyone else.

Anyway it turned out, I was with a bird at the time, and I turned up with her and the money at this pub. But at the same bar was a geezer that later grassed me up. He was one of the actors from the TV show the Fenn Street Gang, who liked to think he could do the same things in real life. There was a dopey bloke in the series who used to say "I'm going to get my tart quite silly." Well I don't know Donnie Barbett, I don't him from Adam, but he recognised me the same way that Snead did, and he said he saw me hand over a parcel to Snead. He put two and two together and grassed me, the bird and Snead.

I was right pissed off when I heard about it, but I have never actually spoken to him about it. Not much point really, he would almost certainly deny it. I mean this is what the police, Detective Inspector Lurkhard at the Yard, told me. He was in the SIB, Special Investigation Branch, so he should have known what happened.

I got a visit from Scotland Yard about police corruption. It stemmed directly about the Bank of America trial. I had to meet someone called DI Griffin from Gravesend nick a couple of times. He wanted to clear his name, as much as I wanted to clear mine, in as much as they were trying to implicate me in the robbery. I had to meet him down at Gravesend at a motel. He was asking questions about a copper called DI Snead who offered for a price to let Johnny go, soon after they arrested him.

The Met was actually after the team for the Bank of America because it happened on their patch. The bloke that caught Johnny however was a bloke from Kent. It got a bit involved it did, with the Kent Police involved because David Mercer in Kent had helped to bury some of Banner's loot for Garthwaite. They were moving around because they were still looking for him. There were reports of a copper being bunged some money, and all this old nonsense. Anyway, Snead offered Johnny a deal, that if he gave him a half a million pounds, half of what he had in his hand in cash, or he could get his hands on, that he'd let him go. But Johnny wouldn't do it, because he didn't trust him.

By now I was being followed all over the place. It was driving me mad. I used to say to them when I spotted them, "Turn round now, I'm going that way," and all this old nonsense, just to wind them up.

I remember taking them to Clapham Junction one day and losing them on purpose. I got them up there to St. John's Hospital. Then I booted the motor, slung a left into the railway, slung a quick right into an alleyway, straight through and out the other side and gone. They came whizzing round the corner because it was a sharpish turn, straight past the alleyway. If there had been anything in the alleyway I'd have been in trouble, but there wasn't, and I wasn't. There was only enough room for one motor to get through. I was down and gone, just to wind them up.

They followed me all over Luton and all over the shop. Things were brought out about police corruption. A10 had to go and visit everybody whose names had been put in the frame. They were part of Operation Countryman.

I will give you just one small example. At one time there was a little firm of people. They were called the 'When They Gonna Do It

Mob.' This little firm used to plan a robbery, well actually they were always planning robberies, as far as I know they're still planning robberies, but they've never yet actually done a robbery.

They used to go outside to the site, radio each other and watch wage deliveries, and so on to see what was occurring. The Old Bill were watching them, and they were watching something they were never going to do.

Anyway this copper turned round to me one day and said that the man from the 'When They Gonna do it Mob' had put me in the frame on something. Anyway they said his name and they said he came out of Fulham. I said, "I know a geezer who thinks he's a bit of a villain, but he's never done anything."

The police were working very hard to implicate me in so many things because they desperately wanted to know about the police corruption pay off business. They wanted me to grass the copper up. That is the way they work. They had to scratch around to find anything they could pin on me to get my attention and cooperation. Which is fair enough if the copper ain't done his duty. And this copper apparently hadn't done his duty. But I never knew enough to put him away anyway.

They kept saying to me, "Don't worry about it, we're not going to implicate you. It's like a jigsaw puzzle: we just want the bits we're missing. The more bits we can get on DI Snead the better."

Nobody likes a bent copper. I think his first name was George. He was, as they say "a known copper that would handle himself." He was like a barrack room lawyer. You could say to him, "Look, I know you took a bribe there," and he'd front it out and get away with it. He took a lot of money off people that man. But I mean what can I do to put him away? My little bit of information won't help. But the A10 Division still made themselves busy.

When the old Bill asked me if I knew Freddie Maiser, I said no, being half truthful, as I don't know him as a friend, except by reputation. Apart from being in his company now, and then and so

I said, "No definitely not." And it still didn't click with me who he was, but I knew him and they got their photographs out, of me, in their company in a pub and so I went, "Who are we talking about then?" They pointed to the photo and said, "But you said you don't know him and there you are talking to him."

I said, "right, I'm in the pub drinking with him, does that mean I know him? I could talk to you but does that mean I know you? We have a habit of talking to people, us British people, we are like that."

He looks at me as if I think I'm some kind of clever dick and went, "I'm not having that!"

I said rather defensively, "Look, I'm telling you, I just happened to be there."

It was in the Butcher's Arms at Battersea, funnily enough. I remember the occasion, I think we were having a benefit 'do' for someone. You know one of those occasions when everyone turned up to show respect, to put in some cash for someone who was locked up, and that was all it was. He was locked abroad, as it goes, in Bangkok. That was tough porridge: if you saw him now you wouldn't recognise him, he is a very different man to what he was. He's still mad, but he isn't the same. As he said, he used to sleep with one eye open, and the stories he tells about it, you know, would make the hair on the back of your neck creep. But to get back to the matter in hand. The police, their knowledge is very comprehensive. You would not believe the sort of details they had, the photos, the faces, the times and dates. This time they had been very thorough.

By now they were getting down to the corruption side of things. So he said, "Well we do know actually that you know a lot of people. We know that you're not an actual, real out and out villain, but you're a part of a circle. In that circle everyone has their uses and you've got your uses, whether it be for getting rid of whatever, or getting motors or whatever it is, you've got a use."

I said, "Flattered I'm sure. You sure you got the right person, you sure it's me? I think you are getting your wires crossed here or somewhere."

So he lets that one lie go, and says, "let's talk about this particular copper Snead. Do you know a DI Snead?"

I lied, "No." He said "Are you sure you don't?" He was writing things down. Then he asked me if I knew Johnny Wilde. He talked a lot about this corruption business, taking me away from the Bank of America, then asked me outright, so I said, "No."

He was trying to find out if I was lying. So then he got one of these Dictaphone things out, and switches on a tape. He said, "Who's that talking on there?"

It said, "All right Johnny how you going, come in." I went, "It could be any other Londoner." "It's you," he says, and of course he is right.

What could I say, "Well, it could be, or it couldn't be. It isn't a very good tape recording, is it?"

He said, "What about this then?" and he opened his briefcase out and he got all these photographs. Then he went, "Who's that?"

This was getting silly, "It's me, what do you mean, who is it?"

He said, "What is that?"

"I don't know." The way he's got all these photographs, all laid out in a set way, it looks as if I've come out of the house and I've looked left and right, then gone over to this car, a Jaguar, and I've looked left and right again. But it's definitely my motor.

So I said, "It's my car, so what, I'm not nicking it."

"Yes, but I asked you if you had ever been to Hedge Lane in Palmers Green, Southgate."

I said, `What, well, I don't remember going there. I don't know every bleeding turning I go in."

"But," he said "You went to Johnny's house."

I thought about it for a few seconds, "Well I don't know nothing about that."

He said, "Well look at these houses here, that's Hedge Lane. Look at this house on the corner." The house that Johnny lived in was on the corner like that, with a turning that suddenly branched off. This corner house, you could have mistaken for being in that turning, instead of part of this big turning, but it wasn't, it was part of Hedge Lane.

Anyway it turned out, that the corner on the other side was an empty house and the coppers were up in the bedroom. There was all this cardboard stuff with holes, pegboard and cameras behind and a microphone fitted so that it could reach across the road here. Everything I said on the doorstep was recorded. They knew I had been to Johnny's house.

So figuring that they had it sewn up, I said, "All right, so I was at Hedge Lane, so I know this man: what's the big deal." I thought, hear it comes, this is where they try to tie me in with the Bank of America job.

But he said, "We're not trying to involve you in anything." And then he started telling me about this tiara, this copper proceeded to tell me about a tiara that was taken over to a house in Ponders End, worth over £300,000 but sold for £83,000.

Well what he's trying to do is, he is trying to frighten me, and he might even have begun to succeed He is trying to let me know that he can nick me any time he likes for my involvement in the Bank of America job.

So I've gone, "I don't know who you're getting your information from, but you've got it wrong and you can't prove that I had anything to do with that."

For good measure, I chuck in, "If you are talking about any one man standing up against me in court, forget it, because it won't stand up."

Just to make it clear to him, I go on, "Because, if you're trying to tell me that someone in the criminal fraternity is going to go the other way on me, without corroborating evidence, you can't do that! Who are they going to believe? Why should they believe him against me?"

By this time I'm getting a little ratty, "What have they got to gain, any jury, or anybody, come to that?"

So then he switches back again, he keeps chopping and changing to keep me off my balance. "Do you every remember meeting a man called DI Snead in the Old Vic pub, it's near the Old Vic theatre."

That's it then, I said "No."

Then he switched again, "Do you know anything about Alex Sears meeting with a policeman." Just in case I didn't know, he adds, "Alex Sears was part of the Thursday Mob." They were the team who went out every Thursday to do a robbery, and got away with it for a long time, before being well and truly grassed.

Now he is diverging, he's really trying to fuck my brain up. He repeated himself, "Do you know anything about Alex Sears meeting with a policeman."

I kept getting visits from all over the place by this DI Lurkhard. I must have had 4 visits to my house from the police, and in the end I said, "Don't keep coming here." They kept coming, and in the end they actually near enough begged me to go to Scotland Yard with them.

They took me into Scotland Yard one day. Actually took me in and signed me in under the name of "Brown," still trying to get the information out of me. I wasn't being obstructive to them. I was helping them as far as I could without incriminating anybody or myself. I was letting things drop that were common knowledge anyway. It wasn't that I was trying to hide anything.

Then they tried to fit me up. They said that this Detective Inspector David Fisk has said that I did this robbery on a security van in

Camden Town. And I had the key made to go in the back door and do it. Now I didn't do it, but they said they were going to fit me up and claim in court that I had done it. They had me down with the right car and everything, all prepared.

I wasn't having any of that. After a while we went up to the 4th floor at Scotland Yard, and there I was sitting there waiting and there's a notice board on the wall there. It's got all my friends' names on it. They tried to box the whole thing in. It just seemed funny that they had six people listed there and I knew three of them quite well. It seemed weird that their names were put up there, unless they were also investigating them at that time.

I never expected at any stage that I would ever get nicked for it, because of the minimal part I played. In the end I did get a pull. I think Old Bill knew, by their checking, names were mentioned, that I was there at the slaughter, it may only have been my first name. Johnny and Willy knew me, Paul knew me. Freddie Maiser I knew, but not so well. He knew me only by my first name, but he wasn't there anyway at the slaughter. He'd been dropped off. What I'm saying is the people who stood for my name, wouldn't have given my name up.

The police afterwards gave me the indication. They even actually said to me, "We know what your part was." Also, "We're not interested in the likes of you." But there was more to this corruption than even I knew about, and they seemed to take that very seriously. It was more than just the deal between Johnny and this DI Snead. There were serious amounts of money not accounted for. Not all of the team got away with their full whack, and what they lost did not always find its way back to the authorities.

Chapter 14 - On the Run

When Jimmy O'Shaughnessy caught the cab in Beak Street, after giving the police the slip at the Great Marlborough Street Magistrates' court on 28th July 1975, he asked the cabbie to drive to High Street Kensington. To throw off any pursuit, and save his small reserves of cash, he got a bus from there to one of his old stamping grounds, Earls Court, home to a dozen expatriate colonies, Irish, Australian, and Arab to name but a few. There he lost himself in the crowd.

Almost as surprised at having escaped as the authorities were, Jimmy was at a bit of a loss as to what to do next. He hadn't actually thought through what he was going to do, he hadn't really dared believe that he would succeed until he actually did it. He needed to contact his girlfriend Jane Spalding, but he knew that would be the first place the police would be watching for him. The longer he hung around, the longer the police had to distribute a picture of him. Jimmy could not even be sure that his picture would not appear in the papers, although he seemed to remember that he was probably safe from this, as he was after all on remand and had not yet actually been found guilty.

Meanwhile Chief Superintendent Jack Slipper was reliving the anguish of losing yet another famous robber. It was bad enough to have lost Ronnie Biggs, but it certainly did not look good for another major robber to have escaped. After ensuring that Jimmy's details were circulated, he went to see Jane Spalding, Jimmy's girlfriend, to see if he could winkle something out of her about Jimmy's whereabouts. He tried to persuade her that the best thing she could do for Jimmy would be to turn him in.

For the next few weeks, Jimmy floated between the city and the country moving from friend's flats to bedsits, and back to supposedly 'safe houses' which cost more than any self-respecting hotel, but which were fronted by 'straight people' who didn't mind earning a bit over the odds for a bit of basic B & B.

For four indecisive weeks he waited, waiting to get hold of some cash either from his Jane or his associates who were minding his stash. Some of the time he spent in Cornwall, using his girlfriend's surname as cover, on what he supposed looked like a golf holiday, but which in fact simply made his lines of contact with her and his London associates even more tenuous. It seemed so pointless just hanging about: now he was free he wanted to get on with the rest of his life.

When at last Jane got some more cash to him, he decided that it was time to make the break now that the heat had died down a bit. Before he left the country he decided to go back to his house in Kingston-upon-Thames and visit his girlfriend. It was going to be some considerable time before she could join him, and in the meantime somebody had to hold down a job. Under the circumstances, with the house being watched for this very reason, returning to Kingston was a very dangerous thing for Jimmy to do, especially as he had worked so hard at making his occasional contact with Jane by phone just about untraceable.

He arrived under cover of darkness, and dropped lightly over the back garden wall. Jane, who had to put up with weeks of cloak and dagger phone box phone calls burst out, "What the hell do you think you are doing here Jimmy O'Shaughnessy. Did I just suffer all these weeks of waiting, just to see you get caught here. Why couldn't we have met somewhere else."

Jimmy was nonplussed at the outburst but soon they found each other's arms and were embracing fit to burst. Jane pulled the curtains in as inconspicuous a way as possible, whilst Jimmy checked his emergency hideout, just in case the police came bursting through the door. He thought he had outwitted them, but you could never tell, specially not with those bastards, the Sweeney.

When Jimmy had been doing up his house he had made one or two little 'improvements' which are not usually to be found on a schedule of works. One of these was a set of floorboards in the cupboard under the stairs, which he prised up, leaving the old nails in them. The cross joists were cut out, and the boards were then hinged so that a man could scramble into the floor cavity space, drop the boards down on himself, and slide some secure bolts on the underside. This meant that the boards looked undisturbed from above, and could not be easily pried up.

Even with close inspection, this particular hideaway would not be detected, unlike some members of the fraternity who have been known to create small rooms for themselves for the same purpose. The later however can be spotted by comparing the size of adjoining rooms, and sussing out what the missing space consists of. Jimmy's little 'priest's hole,' although not very comfortable, was simply part of the expected structure of the house. It was into this hideaway that Jimmy scrambled whenever the door rang, or there were visitors.

Having checked that all was well, they made a simultaneous dive for the stairs, rushed up them and made hard, glorious and noisy love. Jane more than forgave him for the stupid risk he had just taken. Both felt that no matter what happened now they at least had each other. An hour later Jane, feeling much less tense, wandered downstairs and made Jimmy his favourite meal: they eat it in bed.

Next morning they decided that Jimmy would stay there until everything was ready for his departure from the UK. The first hassle was organising a passport. No matter what Frederick Forsythe said in his novel, *The Day of the Jackal*, getting a false passport is not as simple as it sounds. It is much easier to take a real passport belonging to someone of similar height and graft in to it a new photograph.

One time, when I was on the trot, I went to not Spain, but to Belgium on my brother's passport. My photograph, but my brother's name, details and everything. Who knows the difference, I only had his birth certificate and proof that I wanted a passport, plus a photograph of me: fortunately he is only four years younger than me. And there I go, I walked through as him. As he has a different name as well, obviously anyone can do it.

Jimmy however coughed up a fair bit of money and arranged to have it done for him by a specialist, although they did piss him about a bit. Before he had photos done he changed his face by dying his otherwise light hair dark brown and growing a moustache. After messing with the photos and finding even grafting difficult, he finally used someone else's passport, for a fee, which had a photo merely resembling his new looks.

By now he had been in hiding, at considerable cost and with very little achieved, for almost five months. The mere fact of being on the run paralysed all other activity: in some ways it was similar to being locked up in a cell. He couldn't make a move that necessitated being in public places for any length of time. He decided he had to make a move, so he contacted his old mate Freddie Leaf, who had been the architect of the first Bank of America raid, and who had skipped the country in the nick of time. Freddie was living very comfortably near Marbella in Southern Spain. The thought of all that sunshine, cheap booze, lots of golf and real freedom, meant that Freddie didn't have to work very hard to persuade Jimmy that the last place he wanted to be was cold dull London, spending his time skulking behind closed curtains or under floorboards. Jimmy decided to join Freddie, and see what they could plan together: anything to get away from the boredom. Anything to get out into the fresh air, and perhaps play a round or two of golf!

"With your new passport and a different appearance, why don't you simply catch the ferry — there will be hundreds of people about and only a quick passport check," it was Jane trying to deflect Jimmy from his latest death or glory plan. She persisted, "nothing could be more natural, and they won't be expecting you to travel that way."

Jimmy could have simply driven across to France on a cross Channel ferry, which would have been a reasonable course of action, as checks, particularly on the night ferry, of face to passport photo are not that thorough. On the French side the checks were even less thorough. He chose instead to pay a lot more to be taken across the channel at night in a private powerboat by the same Portsmouth to Cherbourg route as the ferry would have taken, but for a much higher fee. Perhaps it was thoroughness, perhaps it was good sense, but on the other hand it might simply have been excessive paranoia.

The plan was for a friend, who often made the crossing to take over a lovely black Jaguar XJ6 with his golf clubs and luggage in the boot, and rendezvous with Jimmy in Cherbourg. From there he planned to drive south to Marbella, Freddie, and freedom.

One night in early January 1975, instead of simply catching the train, Jimmy hired a car and drove down the A3 to Portsmouth, where he met with the power boat owners. Each time he involved more people in his plans, the scope for being grassed up widened. In many ways public transport, especially mass transport, was often far more discreet.

After a couple of close calls, and being thoroughly ripped off by the boat owners for £2,500 he was on his way. Though only an 18 footer the boat cut rapidly through the mercifully gentle swell of the Channel, and after five hours reached Cherbourg. Jimmy seasick and very pissed off at being ripped off, staggered ashore on one of the beaches, and before he had time to turn around the boat was off at full throttle.

He picked up his Jaguar from his friend, cleaned up, had a sleep, and for the first time since leaving the court felt really free.

He motored leisurely south enjoying the French countryside and the pleasures of a good French hotel, till he reached the Spanish border. He need not have feared, the border officials were less interested in his passport than their impending dinner break, and he crossed without incident, using several hitchhikers as additional cover. He continued on down the infamous coast road through Barcelona. The locals drive down this road as if their life depended upon not leaving more than a few feet between their car and the vehicle in front, no matter what speed they are travelling at. Many a tourist has been harassed into making a foolish move by the constant beeping and headlight flashing of the local macho car drivers. The prevalent driving style owes more to Sangria and testosterone than anything else.

After over-nighting in a small town Jimmy continued on towards Tarragona. Growing a bit too confident of the power of his car he pulled out on a steep downwards bend to overtake a slow lorry, and coming suddenly upon the unexpected, managed to smash the Jag into one of those particularly solid Spanish bollards. He was soon being questioned by an over zealous Guardia Civil, one of the many varieties of gun-toting local police officer which Spain had in the 1970s.

Not having arranged any insurance, the famous Green Card, which is no longer necessary for such journeys, he decided that the best thing would be to bribe his way out of the situation and abandon the car. This he successfully did, with some regret, as he was looking forward to driving round Marbella in the Jag. It was a great bird puller wherever it went, but discretion was the better part of valour. He certainly did not want to overnight in a Spanish jail, with the attendant possibility that they might just check up on him with their English opposite numbers.

He headed for Barcelona, and eager to get as far away as possible, caught a local plane to Malaga. From there it was only a rather long taxi ride to Marbella, along a scary cliff road which even after widening had one of the worst traffic accident records in Europe. Here at least it was bright sunshine, and someone else was driving. He lost no time in locating Freddie Leaf's villa.

After a few wrong turnings up steep mountain roads, mostly caused by helpful locals who would sooner give totally wrong directions than admit that they didn't know what the hell you are on about, they located the villa. It was painted white with bougainvillea trailing from its verandah, and had the almost compulsory swimming pool which Spanish builders seemed to knock out with much less fuss, cost and time than their English opposite numbers.

Freddie was not there, so Jimmy paid off the driver, and settled down to wait. It was warm, blessedly warm, and he now had all the time in the world. He had let Freddie stay in his house in Kingston, it was now time for Freddie to return the favour, and offer him a little hospitality. Sunset came and the evening dusk settled in.

"Watcha, are you ever a sight for sore eyes," it was Freddie's booming voice coming out of the velvet darkness.

The two men embraced each other in a way they would not have dreamed of doing on a West End street, Freddie fumbled with his keys, and they were in. It was not till he was having a very generous whisky on Freddie's verandah, and watching the lights of Marbella, that Jimmy felt truly safe. Now he was both free and safe. He sketched out the events of the last few days, and emptied more than a few glasses of Freddie's whisky down his throat.

It didn't take more than a few minutes for them both to forget any plans Jimmy might have had for going back and picking up the Jag: better it stay where it was than that the Guardia Civil should start breathing down their necks. You could never tell with the Spanish police, on the one hand they sometimes looked a fairly dozy bunch, on the other, they were armed to the teeth with pistols and machine-guns.

With less than a year having passed since Generalissimo Franco had been blown up by a car bomb, an explosion which would have impressed even a hardened IRA member, the police and armed forces were more than a little touchy. Spain knew it needed tourists, but did not really know where it was going: it was a sleepy agricultural community being dragged rapidly into the later part of the twentieth century, and unsure if it was going to have another revolution or civil war first.

They talked about the Bank. Freddie was eager to hear how they had in the end cracked it. Jimmy was proud of his job, but all the time he was aware that really it had been Freddie's plan, and Freddie had not even got a drink out of the job. Jimmy implied that it was really Banner who wanted to cut Freddie out. Freddie did not seem to mind: he had been quite active since he had moved to Spain. He was never one to pass up opportunity, and in Marbella opportunity grew on trees.

He moved in a tightly knit community of British expatriates living in and around Marbella. Some of them retirees eking out their pensions in the sun, where they had come when living costs were much lower. Others were members of the fraternity on the run from Old Bill who found the area congenial. Then there was a fair sprinkling of the rich, from a number of countries, who made Marbella their playground, turning up in boats, planes or flash cars. They occasionally involuntarily donated some of their excess wealth to the light fingered gentlemen with whom they often played golf or cards. There was a big trade not only in dope, but also in stolen cars, and hot tom. Interpol also found it a congenial watering hole, for picking up the latest grass intelligence on missing villains or potential jobs.

Further round the coast north of Cartagena was a golf development which although it now belongs to an old and respected shipping company, started life as an exclusive watering hole for American Mafia bosses on enforced furlough in Europe. Such was the easy mix of foreigners in this warm and friendly place. And of course there were the clubs, the restaurants, which even then were still amazingly cheap, the women and the golf. Jimmy went to sleep dreaming of the good times just around the corner.

The next morning Jimmy was about to take a leisurely dip in Freddie's pool, when there was a loud rapping at the door. The Spanish police were there in strength.

"Quick Jimmy, get in here." Freddie pushed him into the all too small airing cupboard, and strode across to the front door.

Freddie swore, "I hope to Christ they don't want to search the place properly. It must have been that fucking taxi driver. If I ever catch up with the ponce..."

Freddie's thoughts stopped in mid-flight as he opened the front door. The officer had on steely reflecting dark glasses — you couldn't read his eyes, but from the set of his mouth he meant business. "Señor Leaf?"

"Si" replied Freddie, trying desperately to remember the Spanish for "I haven't seen him for months."

But the officers did not ask about Jimmy, they just grabbed his wrists and slipped on those thin uncomfortable cuffs, "You are under arrest Señor Leaf, please come with us."

Before he could protest, Freddie was being lead off to the car, and the door slammed, leaving a very confused Jimmy crouching in the airing cupboard, fighting to control his racing heartbeat.

It was almost twenty minutes before Jimmy stirred. He didn't know if it was his lucky day, or the beginning of the end. He tried to think, "What do they want with Freddie. It must be something local. God I hope he doesn't dob me in."

The police obviously wanted Freddie, and Freddie was not one to grass. Come to think of it though, Jimmy had cut Freddie out, at Banner's insistence, of the sweetest tickle ever. Sure he was on the run, but that is because someone had grassed the whole operation, even before Banner started singing.

"No, it couldn't be Freddie, we are mates, aren't we," he thought almost aloud. But what if... well you couldn't be too careful. Should he leave town? He gathered his stuff, found a cab to take him back into Marbella, and booked into a posh hotel right on the waterfront. He was going to tough it out. Besides he was going to need some more money, and that's where the money was, on the wrists and necks and in the pockets of the beautiful people in the hotels on the waterfront.

He cleaned up, called room service, had breakfast, and then sauntered down to one of the bars he remembered as being a bit 'active.' It didn't take him long to find out that Freddie had been taken to Malaga jail. The British police had applied for extradition for his part in the first raid on the Bank of America, and for all those little tickles that he had pulled with Banner. Now Banner, there was a real grass, of that he had been sure for the last three months. Still it seemed aeons ago, so much had happened. He decided to stay in town.

Three days later he bumped into someone who had been in close contact with Freddie, a guy called Bernie. Apparently the British cozzers were due to arrive at the weekend. Typical that, he thought, the Met wouldn't let them come down to Malaga during the week, they might just enjoy themselves a bit too much. Might cause a little envy in the ranks.

Freddie had asked Bernie to get together some scratch in a hurry. Bernie had been liquidating one or two of Freddie's prizes. The local fences were even meaner when you were in trouble. Anyway before the weekend arrived, Freddie has greased a few Spanish palms with the equivalent of ten year's wages and is taken, by police car would you believe, late one night to the Algeciras ferry. By morning he is in Morocco where Britain has no extradition treaty. He asked Bernie to give Jimmy a short and cryptic message.

As you can imagine, Jimmy felt as if his plans had been shot to pieces. What to do now? Somehow the whole point of being in southern Spain had evaporated. "What if they have figured out that I am in Marbella as well and apply for my extradition?"

Jimmy though for a while about following Freddie to Morocco, but Spain was really about as foreign as he wanted to be, and anyway being with Freddie might be more dangerous than being a loner. He hit upon the idea of traveling north to Galicia, a corner of Spain that the tourists did not reach. Cooler in both senses of the word.

A train ride later he was comfortably set up in a friend's house on the colder stormy north Atlantic coast of Spain. Gone were the flash and the rich of Marbella, as were all those tempting golf clubs. Jimmy reasoned that it would be much safer: he had hardly spent two weeks in southern Spain.

Safer but boring. Here in the cold Jimmy sunk into a withdrawn frame of mind and began to drink heavily. He wondered what exactly he was doing there: his missed his friends and Jane. He could not even make any money here. After one bar room brawl too many, it became difficult to find somewhere to drink. What to do? He decided to pack his bag and head back to England, after all what was the point. He might be safe from the cozzers here, but it was good for very little else, except perhaps cheap booze, and now he couldn't even drink that in the local boozers.

After all the cost and care taken in escaping from England, he decided simply to rely upon his passport and take a package flight from Madrid to Gatwick, from where he planned to catch public transport to Kingston. Not exactly the return of the conquering hero, but what else could he do?

Jane's first reaction was less than reassuring. "What the bleeding hell do you think you are doing. We spend all that money to get you safely out of England, you get bored in Spain in less than a month, and you come back as if you were any old tourist. For God's sake don't you realise that the police are looking for you, and they mean to lock you up and throw away the key?"

Jimmy's first reaction was "ungrateful bitch, I came back because I was missing you," and after a pause he added, "and to beat some sense into those ungrateful bastards sitting on a pile of my money."

Jane could see it was no use, and soon they reverted to the old routine, keeping the hiding place ready for any sound of a visitor. After a while their guard began to slip. A few unguarded words one evening over dinner to someone they thought was a mate, and the next minute the place was swarming with cozzers who knew exactly where to look under the stairs. Jimmy was back in custody on the 10th April 1976, just eight and a half months after he escaped. In some ways he was relieved — at least now life might be boring, but it would be predictable.

Meanwhile Freddie Leaf was living quite pleasantly in an old and slightly run down hotel near the main square in Tangiers. The weather was warm, the people were laid back and the hash was cheap. A leather factory was a short distance away. The smell of leather, the still warm evenings, a modicum of the excellent local hashish and an occasional impressionable female tourist passed the time pleasantly enough. Freddie liked the slow pace of life, it gave him plenty of time to think, and Freddie liked to think. The Moroccans had not yet got into the habit of plaguing the tourists, and Freddie was not the sort of person anyone bothered just for the fun of it. He was later to move up to Marrakech and move for a while into the fabulous Marmounia Hotel, but that was after several rather successful evening forays in Tangiers.

It was from here that he heard the news of Jimmy's re-arrest in London. Why had he returned to London? He guessed Jimmy never felt as relaxed in foreign places as he did. Freddie had first been to Morocco at the high spot of the hippy culture in the late sixties, and although the infernal tourists had begun to ruin the place, he remembered the old hands like Paul Bowles, for whom Tangiers was home. And who was that young rather good looking youth he had with him, whose name reminded Freddie of one of the great London Squares? Even some of Hollywood's greats and the likes of Barabara Hutton had houses, or in some cases palaces, in Morocco.

Freddie enjoyed Morocco, and was still there in November 1976, but soon after he decided to move on, as Morocco had got too hot for him. He was after all very easy to spot, and for Freddie's line of work you needed to blend into the surroundings. Freddie flew to West Germany, but did not find it as congenial as he had hoped. The Germans were just a mite to well organised for his liking. A spot of winter sports might not be a bad idea, and anyway that was where the money was at this time of year. He took a train to Austria where he was soon up to a few nice little tickles in Kitzbuhel, one of the high class ski resorts.

In February 1977, using the identity of William Nicholl, Freddie pulled off an armed robbery in the Lebenberg Palace Hotel, one of the main hotels in Kitzbuhel. The job had Freddie Leaf's signature all over it, and like the Bank of America, involved safety deposit boxes. The night porter of the hotel was bound and gagged and the safe deposit boxes containing valuables which belonged to the guests were canned open and emptied. The theft of jewels and cash amounted conservatively to £130,000. Before long the police had marked Freddie's card and were moving in. Austria was getting too hot for him: he had been there for only five months.

In May 1977 he decided that he needed a little sun and had moved on to Greece, just hours ahead of arrest in Austria, where he was joined by his wife Sheila. Interpol however spotted him, and he was picked up by the Greek police.

Both Austria and Scotland Yard made an attempt to extradite him. When they picked him up, the Greek police asked for his passport. He made his first mistake when he offered them the passport of Jimmy William Nicholl. As it turned out this was a distinctly bad move, as the Greek police arrested and charged him with a false declaration of identity, and entering Greece under an assumed name. On 2 July 1977 he was found guilty by an Athens court, and sentenced to a seven month prison sentence, or a £680 fine. He decided to serve the time rather than pay the fine. Freddie's luck was beginning to run out.

Two weeks later while Freddie was still in jail, the Athens Appeal court began hearing both governments' requests to extradite him, each in connection with a robbery. He had been in tougher corners, and remained cool. Freddie prided himself on being able to survive under most conditions, and come up smiling.

On 18 July 1977 the Athen's court ruled that the British extradition order was valid, but adjourned to hear the Austrian case. Scotland Yard wanted Freddie on six charges, one of which related to the first abortive burglary attempt on the Bank of America, the other five included defrauding Christie's of jewellery worth £240,000. There were other charges, but these they reasoned should be enough to secure extradition.

Freddie knew on which side his bread was buttered and told journalists at the trial about the notoriously tough Greek jails, "They are treating me marvelously. They are looking after me admirably well." Obviously a short stay in a Greek prison was certainly preferable to two long stays in British and Austrian prisons. His wife Sheila was with him in court, and was trying through a local lawyer, Alexander Lykourezos to have the extradition orders overturned by contending that British evidence was inadmissible in a Greek court of law.

By 9 August the court had accepted the validity of both extradition orders, and Freddie's appeal had gone to the Greek Supreme court. Freddie's lawyer insisted that the Supreme court rule irrevocably within eight days on both extradition requests. The final decision as to if, or where, Freddie was to be extradited was down to Mr. Constantine Stefanakis, the Greek Minister of Justice.

The problem for the Minister was that if he agreed to Britain's request then Austria would be unable to extradite him later, because no country will allow the extradition of its own citizens. On the other hand Freddie could have been tried in Britain for offences committed in Austria. Freddie and Sheila were both hoping that the Greeks would choose the course of inaction rather than making a decision, allowing the deadline to pass.

The hearing, scheduled for 16 August was postponed because of the illness of Freddie's lawyer. Freddie refused to be represented by a court appointed solicitor, hoping probably to force the court into a favourable decision, due to his lack of representation. The hearing was again postponed.

Finally Freddie's appeal was rejected. Freddie reckoned that he could possibly beat the rap on the Bank of America charge, but knew he could then not be extradited to Austria, so he said that he did not oppose the British extradition order because he wanted to "fight the charges" however he said that he opposed the Austrian extradition order.

On 13 September 1977 the Greek Minister of Justice was to thwart Freddie's plans by granting the Austrian extradition order. Worse still, the Greek court ruled that whatever happened he had to serve the rest of his 7 month sentence for using a false identity.

Two days later Scotland Yard switched its extradition request from Greece to Austria, in case Freddie somehow managed to get off the Kitzbuhel armed robbery charge. Two days later Freddie arrived in Vienna under armed guard.

Freddie was put on trial for the armed robbery in the Lebenberg Palace Hotel at Kitzbuhel in February 1977. He pleaded guilty to aiding and abetting the robbery, but denied being personally involved. Clutching at straws, Freddie reckoned that he had been blackmailed into helping two men do the robbery when they threatened to reveal his false identity to the Austrian police. Freddie said he had allowed the men to use a rented house in Kitzbuhel for cover, and showed then where to hide the rifled steel boxes they had taken from the hotel safety deposit lockers. He also said he had sold them his car, and at the time of the robbery it did not belong to him. Freddie was skating on thin ice, and the Austrian prosecutor knew it. There was virtually no part of the planning of the robbery that Freddie was not involved in. Further, he claimed to have received no part of the proceeds of the robbery.

It took the jury of six men and two women just three hours on 25 April 1978 before they decided unanimously that they did not believe him. Judge Walter Murr handed down a nine year sentence for his part in the robbery. Freddie casually replied that, "It seems rather a long time doesn't it?" Under common Austrian practice, Freddie could expect to serve at least a third of the sentence.

His lawyer immediately lodged two appeals, one for the annulment of the trial and another against the harshness of the sentence.

On 26 April 1978, in an Innsbruck court, the same Austrian Judge ruled that the British extradition application would be enforced when Freddie finally was released from the sentence passed on him for the robbery in Kitzbuhel.

Freddie served his three years, and was extradited to London where he was remanded at Marlborough Street Magistrates' court on 1 November 1981, charged with seven offences. This was the same court that Jimmy O'Shaughnessy had escaped from back in 1975.

One year later, when the case finally came to trial, Freddie pleaded not guilty of conspiracy to burgle the Bank of America. He also pleaded not guilty to a further six charges including that of robbing two antique shops in Kingston and Chelsea in 1971 and 1972, and the charge of dishonestly obtaining jewellery worth £240,00 from Christie's in 1975, using bogus bank drafts.

Freddie must have been in luck, for Mr. Stephen Mitchell, the same barrister who had prosecuted Banner said that the Crown, "After long and careful reflection would offer no evidence on the charges."

Quite how Freddie managed that I don't know. The prosecution's "quite exceptional course," with which the judge apparently agreed, occurred because it was fairly certain that Stewart Banner would not be tempted to show his nose in open court again. By then Banner would have been given a totally new identity by the police and would be unwilling to endanger his life simply to help the prosecution of Freddie Leaf, a man he knew was quite capable of catching up with him and exacting revenge. In addition Freddie's lawyers could easily demonstrate some untruths in Banner's testimony.

So Freddie, who was the original moving force behind the whole idea of the Bank of America job, walked to freedom on 5 November 1981. Outside the court Freddie said, "It is a tremendous relief to be at liberty, and not to have the constant worry of looking over my shoulder. The past is behind and I am able to plan for the future for the first time in many years."

What happened to the others who had not gone on the run?

Rejoined by Jimmy O'Shaughnessy they were still languishing in, Brixton Prison almost a year after their arrests. To find out we have to turn back to June 1976.

Chapter 15 - Trial and Sentencing

It was not till 10th June 1976 that the rest of the accused were tried, most having been held on remand during the more than a year that the case took to come to trial. I suppose the police figured that given that they had not retrieved much of the proceeds of the robbery, that the main men were quite likely to do a runner.

At the trial itself, they cross-checked the identity of everybody who went to the public gallery. Not everybody was allowed in. The same happened with the Thursday mob trial, when they got done. I said to my missus "you shouldn't go to the trial." But because there was so much conflict between Susie Hillyard and this bird Viv, Johnny Wilde's wife, she went to the trial anyway. She knew both of them and wanted to see what happened: she liked a bit of a spat. And of course she got her name taken. Nothing ever came of it fortunately, but you never know. But I wouldn't have gone. Nothing easier for the police than to have a ready made list of suspects, of people interested in the trial.

I had got someone else who was at the trial, most of the time to tell me what was going on. He kept going in and relaying information back to me, watching to see if I had in any way been implicated. But they couldn't get in every day. Visitors to the Public Gallery at the Old Bailey were so strenuously vetted and you had to be careful who went in and who came out. It didn't do to appear too often on the police's list of interested parties. To be quite honest with you, I wasn't really all that concerned. To me it was just a day and a half's work, and I relied upon Johnny not to grass me up.

The trial began on Friday 10th June 1976. On the first morning there was a little drama. One of the accused got shot on his way to the Old Bailey.

The Mayfair Bank Job

On the morning of the trial, several men in dark coats were seen hanging around All Saints' Church from where they had a good view of Johnny O'Connell's house in Church Vale, East Finchley. Less than a minute after he had left his home, as O'Connell turned into Twyford Avenue, one of the men purposely approached him and calmly shot him in the back of the left leg with a sawn-off shotgun. The men disappeared down a footpath behind the church into Durham Road where a car was waiting for them. O'Connell collapsed on the ground in a rapidly growing pool of blood. He was rushed to hospital and surgeons were doubtful if they could save the leg as it had been pretty effectively messed up. After several operations they eventually amputated it.

Johnny O'Connell, a company director and launderette operator aged 41, had been charged with conspiracy to rob the Bank of America. Obviously someone was keen to impress it upon him that he shouldn't talk about his fellow defendants, and they paid someone to have a pop at him. Several days earlier several men had been seen attempting to verbally change his mind about testifying.

He had apparently been doing a lot of 'shopping,' and so they had to pay to have him done. Such men are not hard to get hold of, and fairly cheap, compared to the threat a long prison sentence.

Normally this would smack either of a fairly desperate defendant, or a bit of creative interference from the East End mob that had a marginal interest in the job. However a woman rang the police, not the ambulance, to tell them about the shooting, and then disappeared. Newspapers at the time linked this woman with one of the female defendants, without naming names. Perhaps coincidentally, Viv Wilde, wife of Johnny Wilde was later warned by the judge in the trial, that any 'accidents' occurring to other witnesses would be laid squarely at her door.

Who knows, perhaps Johnny O'Connell was about to spill the beans on the real grass in the case, the grass who had alerted the police before the actual night of the job. The trial started without Johnny O'Connell. It was going to be a long couple of months in hospital for him.

Nobody was ever brought to trial over the shooting. O'Connell did not in the end testify, but pleaded guilty to involvement in the planning of the first raid, of "conspiring to enter the Bank of America in Davies Street, between June 1 and October 28, 1974, as a trespasser with intent to steal." This means that O'Connell was only concerned with the first abortive raid, and may in fact have been one of the lock or alarm experts which Leaf originally got Banner to show round the bank. When O'Connell was finally tried in December 1977 the prosecution accepted that he had already undergone more than enough punishment as a result of the shooting, and simply asked for a suspended sentence.

The same newspaper report (*Times*, 12 June 1976) described the case as "one of the biggest bank robberies in history." The trial started with 100 potential jurors. It took an hour to select the jury because of 29 challenges from the defense, plus a further 39 exemptions given because of the likely length of the trial. This was estimated to run 6 to 10 weeks. In the event the trial ran for more than 13 weeks. The court finally selected 11 men and one woman. Each night the jury were given a plainclothes police escort to and from court because the authorities feared that with that amount of cash still floating around, the bribing or threatening of a jury member would be a relatively easy task.

The presiding Judge was the same one who tried Banner in September 1975, his Honour Judge King-Hamilton, QC, and he was therefore well versed in the events of that fateful evening. All the accused denied every charge. They all had well crafted alibis. None of them could believe that such a perfect robbery had been so thoroughly grassed up. They came to court at the Old Bailey, if you can imagine, sitting in black mohair suits and polo neck jumpers, all looking exactly what they were.

Michael Worsley appeared for the prosecution, and said that the raid had involved more than £2 million in cash jewellery and bullion, still far short of the actual amount. He also stated that a

The Mayfair Bank Job

total of £300,000 had been recovered. Eventually the authorities were to recover a mere £500,000 from the robbery.

He went on to outline the already familiar history of the two attempts on the Mayfair branch, one a failure, the other a success. Banner was then introduced as the main prosecution witness. Despite the fact that Banner had been kept apart from other prisoners, under Rule 43, in Wandsworth Prison, to prevent them getting at him for his grassing, there were several 'incidents' in which Banner was abused and had filth thrown at him. Some prison warders were also encouraged, by the others, to make life difficult for Banner. By the time came for him to stand up in court and give his damning evidence, he was much less certain that he had chosen the right course of action. Much of his testimony was directed towards trying to persuade the jury that he was just a poor misguided wretch who had been taken advantage of by the professional robbers in the dock.

The prosecutor's easiest cross-examination was Willy Gavroche, who was faced with the parking ticket which he had received just near the Bank of America at 5 pm on the day in question. Although he initially denied all charges, Willy could see that his alibi was blown, and that Banner had already destroyed any chances the gang might have had of acquittal, so he made a complete admission. Having been convinced by the police to give back £125,000 (although some said £500,000 had been returned by him), he held out hope for a reduced sentence. He had to wait more than 13 weeks to learn what that would be. In the meantime he spent his time clowning around in the dock, secure he thought, in the knowledge that his sentence would not be very great.

Being a natural comic, with a talent for ventriloquism, he was soon throwing his voice so that some of the barristers, and the stuffier witnesses appeared to be saying the most outrageous things. When the judge wanted to know who said that, it was never Willy, who was always studiously looking the other way, or staring at the ceiling with rapt attention. Willy Gavroche was too funny for his own good. The comical things they were saying and doing were not lost on the Judge, who probably felt that the affront to the dignity of the court was a greater offence than the robbery itself.

Pointing to one of the prosecutors, Willy would ask, `Does he sleep in the fucking suit or what." Later Willy turns to Paul and says, "See that bird up in the public gallery, third one on the right, she fancies me." Getting into the spirit of the thing, Willy waves to her and begins to make a thrusting motion.

The others resisted quite such an easy victory for the prosecution.

Johnny Wilde, who was tried under his real name had unfortunately been flashing his newly acquired wealth round the day after the robbery.

He and his wife Viv had had a real ding-dong argument after Johnny came in late on the morning after the night of the robbery. In a sort of self-protective desperation he had offered to buy her a new kitchen, just to shut her up, and stop her going on. After all he could now afford it. He was dog tired, but after a bath, a change of clothes and a quick bite to eat, they jumped in the car went shopping down at Hendon.

Viv and he finally settled upon one particular kitchen in a furniture shop. Johnny reached the desk, and was a bit pissed off when one of the jumped up assistants turned away from him to serve someone else who only wanted some carpet tape. "I'll show the little creep' he said under his breath, and pulled a wad of notes out of the pocket of his jacket and peeled off £1,015 for the kitchen units. With a flourish he plumped the wad down on the counter and asked the assistant if he could now spare some of his precious time for a serious customer. He thought back to the time he had cleaned out another but similar store not very far from here, just because the sales assistant had been so irritatingly pompous that he wouldn't let him have a discount for cash. He hated stuck up counter jumpers: manners didn't cost a lot.

The assistant not only noticed Johnny's gesture, but remembered that "he put back in his pocket about as much as he had paid out" when he subsequently came to testify in court. The prosecution seemed to think that carrying this much cash around, in those days, was as good as a confession. The jury, for whom that amount of money might have been half a years' wages, were inclined to agree. Johnny was openly contemptuous in court of this testimony, saying that he often carried this amount of cash with him. The jury looked a little skeptical. The prosecution pressed on.

The police had picked over Johnny's house with a fine tooth comb. Of course, under a few loose floorboards and in the shed at the back they found tools for copying precision made keys, and a number of locks lying round carelessly on a bench. No direct connection with the robbery could be proved, but you could see that the jury understood the significance of this evidence.

Meanwhile Viv had been arrested shortly after the police had searched Johnny's home. They had found 19 £20 notes in her handbag, which they contended came from the robbery. She was formally charged was dishonestly receiving and dishonestly handling money known to have come from a robbery. She loudly protested her innocence, but privately wished she had spent more than £120 of the money Johnny had thrust into her hand the morning of their argument after the robbery.

In the end Viv was one of the few accused to receive a not guilty verdict. She did however spend more than 6 months on remand before they let her go. They realised that they could get to Johnny through her, and that she was much more interested in saving her own skin than that of her husband's.

The prosecution barrister, Michael Worsley asked Johnny what he had been doing on the night of 24 April 1975. Johnny's first alibi was that he had spent the night at home with his wife and daughter, during which a visitor called in briefly. However, his wife Viv, who had obviously thought a great deal during her months on remand, decided that getting too involved with her husband's nocturnal activities that night might not be so good for her own immediate future and long-term freedom. When called to the witness stand she simply said she had not seen him from lunch time on one day till almost lunchtime the next day.

Johnny was gobsmacked. After a quick consultation with his brief, he decided to let the court have his 'real' alibi, a night of passion with Susie Hillyard. He knew that at least she would back him up. It even sounded natural that as a concerned husband he should protect his wife from this knowledge till she too let him down badly in court. Vivienne, who was not immune from the occasional bout of histrionics, immediately let fly at her hapless husband, screaming insults at both him and his supposed bed companion of the night.

It all fitted in quite nicely till Viv's threats became rather too graphically earnest, and the Judge remembered back to what had happened to Johnny O'Connell on the very first day of the trial. Order was eventually restored.

The Judge gave a strong warning to Viv, that if anything happened to Susan Hillyard, the court would hold her responsible, even if she 'accidentally' fell over and broke her arm. Johnny wondered what the jury had made of all this and wished that his wife hadn't enjoyed her role quite so much. He did rather like the occasional evenings he had snatched with Mrs. Hillyard, even if the night in question had not been one of them.

With his alibi on shaky ground, Johnny was then administered the *coupe de grace* by the prosecution. Banner was called and identified Johnny as the person he had, at Freddie Leaf's suggestion, taken down to the vault doors on several evenings before the first raid. He said he showed Johnny the vault and the alarm cupboard, which Johnny had unlocked with 'a piece of metal.' There was not really much that Johnny could say except steadfastly deny Banner's statement. Johnny Wilde was found guilty of conspiracy to burgle the bank and also of robbing it.

The first verdicts came out on the 10th November, 1976, the ninetieth day of the trial, but 152 days after the trial had begun, allowing for court recesses and holidays. The rest of the verdicts were read on the 12th November. The jury spent two nights locked up in a nearby hotel under guard, whilst they decided. Most of the jurors were well relieved that the trial was over. The trial itself was estimated to have cost the crown £500,000. Less than that was recovered. It was another four days before the judge passed sentence on 16th November.

Despite putting up a good fight, Paul Caldwell, who had not been allowed bail, was convicted of robbery, but not guilty of conspiracy to burgle the bank. I guess the jury thought that Paul had not contributed very much to the planning.

The police knew that Paul had stashed his loot somewhere quite clever, and were determined to find it. When they raided Paul Caldwell's house they devastated it and did a lot of damage, they ripped up his floor boards, they emptied his swimming pool, and took all the tiles off the walls inside the swimming pool. They may have had a tip off, but if so it didn't tally with reality. The police tore his extension to pieces, took tongue and groove off the wall, opened up the drains, and pulled out all the ceiling insulation. They felt there had to be something there so they just ripped it to pieces.

The two who drew the longest sentences were Johnny Wilde (23 years) and Paul Caldwell (21 years). In both cases no money was handed back, so after inflicting sentences in excess of that meted out for multiple murder or treason, the authorities decided to also take criminal bankruptcy proceedings against these two, for the sum of £485,000. In the judge's view, because of the amount taken, this was not a 'normal' crime and therefore warranted abnormally harsh sentences.

This meant that the authorities could, and did, take away houses and assets belonging to both of them even before the date of the robbery. This meant Johnny's house in Devonshire Road, Palmers Green and Paul's home in Meadway, Southgate were taken. The authorities were determined to make these two suffer as much for what they did, as for what they would not tell.

Willy Gavroche was persuaded to give back £125,000 which he claimed was all he had. Willy who thought that giving back some money would put him in good odour with the police, was shocked to receive an 18 year sentence. Hardly worth giving back the money to get a lousy 3 years knocked off the sentence. He had been found guilty of robbing the Bank (technically of robbing a bank employee), but Judge King-Hamilton discharged the jury from bringing in a verdict on the alternative but lesser charge of burglary.

Jimmy O'Shaughnessy had been well lollied by Banner, and the police had recovered some of his loot. His escape also was very much against him, so on the advice of his solicitors, Baldwin Mellor and Company he pleaded guilty. They briefed Victor Durand QC to make his plea of mitigation. O'Shaughnessy, who had been picked up again after almost one year at liberty following his break from Marlborough Street Magistrates' court, had to wait till the whole trial had ended before he heard his sentence. He was sentenced to 17 years. Some of the other team members felt that this lower sentence indicated that Jimmy, like Banner had been grassing. Perhaps the slightly lower sentence reflected a degree of cooperation with the police, but it is more likely that it was simply his plea of guilty.

Jimmy's girlfriend, Jane Spalding who was charged with "unlawfully attempting to pervert justice by harbouring him," was discharged on 10 April 1976. Of course she did hide her boyfriend 'with intent to impede his arrest and prosecution' as the court documents put it, in their extremely clever 'priest's hole' under the floorboards off their hall cupboard, but who could blame her.

The strangest sentence handed out was that of Jeffrey Houdan who received 12 years, after he had obligingly pleaded guilty to dishonestly receiving. He was actually accused of receiving £1,862 and $4,961 and some jewellery. It is extraordinary that a sentence for receiving stolen property of twelve 12 years, was in fact greater than that normally handed out for murder. Obviously the police thought that Jeffrey had received a major part of the proceeds of the robbery.

Mickey Jevons, who had been out enjoying himself on bail, was convicted of conspiracy to burgle the Bank of America, but only in connection with the first abortive attempt. Nobody attempted therefore to grill him as to the whereabouts of his share of the proceeds from the second raid. Because of this, and possibly for his cooperation, he drew a mere 18 months sentence.

Apart from Freddie Maiser who was never arrested, that accounted for all the main gang members.

Johnny's wife, Viv was found not guilty of dishonestly handling money known to have been stolen. She later had a further two specimen charges of receiving in connection with the robbery dropped. In return the police were left in possession of more information than they previously had. Despite her earlier behaviour, when she was acquitted she collapsed into her husband's arms, and left the court crying with relief. She made so much noise that she didn't hear Judge Hamilton-King's comment on her case, "before you leave the court, there is something I would like to say to you."

The Judge was not going to allow her outburst to drown his warning. When she had recovered outside the court she was brought in again and Judge King-Hamilton said, "I just want to say this to you, and please regard it as a solemn warning. If anything happens to Mrs. Hillyard as a result of what you do or what you cause others to do, as a result of the evidence she has given in this court, then you can expect no mercy at all." Susan Hillyard, who was 35, had given Johnny the alibi evidence he needed, but after hearing Viv's outbursts had written to the police saying she feared for her safety.

Edward 'Tag' Garthwaite, who had helped Banner hide his loot admitted dishonestly handling £32,810 and $25,500 and jewellery and was given a 2 year sentence.

The East End contact Johnny Jimmy Mason, who had been out on bail, was found not guilty of conspiracy and discharged. He was of course supplied with the very best criminal barrister. The other defendant from the East End of London, Harold Scott, had already been discharged before the main trial started.

Jeffrey Stitcher was found guilty of dishonestly handling proceeds from the bank robbery, specifically £2,500 and one Krugerrand, and received a 3 year sentence. His connection with Johnny via the greengrocery fraternity had ensured that.

Another of the defendants, George Birmingham, aged 36, a carpenter of Ongar, Essex, was found not guilty of dishonestly receiving £1,500 from the robbery, because the prosecution could not adequately establish a connection between him and the robbery.

Another early defendant, David Mercer, the 27 year old civil servant who lived in Brenchley in Kent was discharged. Freddie Leaf who planned the original raid must have been laughing up his sleeve, living comfortably under an assumed name in North Africa at the time of the trial.

In all over 104 years of prison sentences were handed out.

A sequel to the above events occurred in late April 1977. As a result of a series of raids in south London culminating in an ambush at Beckenham Junction by the police of an armoured security van robbery in progress, the police arrested 18 people. Two of those picked up were wanted in connection with the robbery of the Bank of America.

In the end after their appeal on 24th February 1978 seven of those convicted in the second trial had their sentences reduced by between one and four years. The final sentences, with the reduced term in brackets, in order of length were:

Johnny Wilde	23 (20)
Paul Caldwell	21 (18)
Willy Gavroche	18 (15)
Jimmy O'Shaughnessy	17 (14)
Jeffrey Houdan	12 (8)
Stewart Banner	7

Jack Stitcher	3 (2)
Edward Arthur Garthwaite	2
Mickey Jevons	18 months

As Jeffrey Stitcher had already served 2 years by this time he was immediately released. Mickey Jevons was refused leave to challenge his conviction. Most of the others could expect to serve 2/3rds of their new sentences with good behaviour. Johnny, Paul and Willy were treated as category 'A' prisoners, which is the highest security. All have now been released with the last, Johnny Wilde, coming out in 1991.

Where most of money went was certainly not resolved by the trial. In his summing up Judge King-Hamilton, QC said "what has been concealed will remain salted away so far as you are concerned for a great many years." Certainly the judge never discovered what happened to all that money.

Chapter 16 - Buried Treasure

Eventually the authorities were to recover a mere £500,000 from the robbery. That much was spent by them on the trial alone. This means that those who did not return any of their gear had time to stow it away, although some used some of it for their escape (Jimmy O'Shaughnessy), their legal defense (Johnny Wilde) and other less worthy purposes. Some definitely ended up in the hands of bent policemen, something that is bound to happen with such enormous sums involved.

What to do with the loot is a perennial problem. If it's hot tom, recently stolen, then a fence is not going to give you more than one tenth of its value. Even cash in large quantities is hard to deal with. Say if you got off today with £800,000 in cash, or at today's values considerably more, with more than a few bits of classy jewellery, where would you put it? Think about it.

Now you don't want to keep it in your house because if you get a spin from the cozzers, because of your known associates, then you've had it. As Paul Caldwell's case proved, the police are not averse to totally tearing up your house, if they think you have hidden something they want to find. Paul got out in 1987 or 1988, and has kept a low profile since.

Another possibility is putting it in a safety deposit box, for god's sake. Hopefully, one that is not going to get turned over by somebody else! One of the team deposited his gear in his box in the Chancery Lane Silver Vaults as soon as he could, figuring that it would be safer there than most places. The police however have a habit of finding out if you've got a safety deposit box, unless you plan it so very, very well and rent it well beforehand. They can even check informally if you have opened it recently, as each time a customer opens his box the fact is recorded by the bank or security company. Some of the money taken during the Wembley bank raid in the early 1970s for example was later retrieved by the police from such a safe deposit belonging to one of the robbers.

Small boxes only cost £100 or £150 a year. In Selfridges boxes used to be only £150 a year. Of course if you had as much jewellery as Johnny had, after he had bought it from the other members of the team, even several large boxes would be hard pressed to hold it. It makes a lot of sense. But, you have to sort of sit down and figure it out beforehand. You have to have a criminal mind or expectations to organise it.

If a villain, with a box or a buried stash gets killed or shot, or whatever, he's either been clever enough to leave a letter or something somewhere such as with a solicitor for someone to get hold of, for example his wife, or he dies and nobody gets anything, because nobody knows where he has put his stash. Obviously he is going to think twice about committing these details to paper.

It's the hardest thing in the world to look after money. Even legitimate money needs an army of so called investment advisors. There are three basic solutions for bent money. One is burying it, whether in the ground or figuratively in another vault. The second is taking it out of the country, a lot more difficult in the mid-1970s than now with the lifting of many banking and border controls. The third is putting it to work in a business. Several well-known robbers have provided severe headaches for their auditors by injecting bent money into their businesses. Others like Johnny, have entrusted some of the cash to business associates, who have been less than creative businessmen.

All the other more sophisticated laundering operations are too expensive and not really open to members of the fraternity who have a one off big windfall gain. It's OK for the drug smugglers: they have the time to set up the necessary dummy corporations, to recycle the money back into business, and protect it from prying eyes. Their operation is more like regular import-export activity, for which they deposit their profits outside the reach of the authorities, and get banks to supply them with back-to-back loans in their country of operation to continue financing their business. For the average 'active' member of the fraternity, who occasionally makes a good score, he usually relies upon his mates. However if he gets banged up for say 20 years, like the Bank of America team, then even the closest mate must be tempted to help himself.

On the whole if people are burying stuff, it will be in public places rather than in their homes, so that if it's found it cannot be traced back to them. Or for a bit more privacy, somebody else's field, although that leaves them open to other problems. In Johnny's case, one of his associates who had a field in Essex, died before Johnny got out of jail and reclaimed his gear. Johnny had contacts in Essex, and there was some talk about him burying some of the tom in a field in Essex, with Mickey Flynn. Mickey Flynn however died in July 1987, before Johnny got out.

One of the terrible things about burying the loot is coming back years later to find it cemented over, or that water has got to it and it's gone all mouldy. You might even bury it where it could later be excavated or a block of flats could be built over it when you come back.

In addition, the government regularly deliberately changes the design of the currency, not just to save the Mint's printing bills by reducing the size of the paper that notes are printed on, but to discourage forgers and to make it difficult for anyone to unearth large quantities of old notes years after they have been taken out of circulation, and then to use them. One of the Great Train Robbers had great difficulty in disposing of stacks of old ten shilling notes which had not only gone mouldy, but were just about to go out of circulation in the early 1970s. It took frantic trips to various small banks round the country with various cock and bull stories about why the money had gone mouldy, to change it into current pound notes.

When Gordon 'Checker' Goody tried to change the ten shilling notes from the Great Train Robbery, he and his mates had first to dig it up from its resting place on Wimbledon Common, and near the common at the bottom on Lower Richmond Road, near Lower Richmond Road Hospital. When it was buried all the turf was put back. It was put in polythene bags in a box. However a lot of damp did penetrate through and destroyed some of the notes. We then went to Manchester and Birmingham and many other towns, changing the money. We had to answer a lot of questions, by saying it was 'in an old cupboard' or a biscuit tin, and other stories. Of course each time we had to be sure to only change quantities that would not raise suspicions. Nevertheless a lot of questions were asked.

As for taking it overseas, to a country like Switzerland and putting it in a bank there, well that is for people who are in the know: the rich who know how to look after their money, and how to act properly in a foreign bank. But you're talking about people who know these things and who are successful. The others, regular crooks, never had that amount of money to even contemplate putting it into an overseas bank, a local safety deposit maybe.

The few major robbers who did move their money out of the country, paid supposedly respectable folk between 5 and 10% to do it for them. Some were even hit for 20% for the simple service of driving the cash over a few borders, or transmitting it through banking channels under the guise of a bogus commercial transaction. This was paying through the nose really, after all the Swiss never stopped anyone coming into their country with suitcases stuffed with money, and even Britain doesn't usually check cases on the way out, particularly if it's a package holiday. Providing the name you are using isn't tapped into one of the computers that immigration has, you are nobody, even if you are going into Switzerland.

If you travel on your own passport though, they can check you on their computer. Then they ask the banks if anybody in the last eighteen months has opened a deposit account a box. Most villains have had their deposit accounts in other names, or a safety deposit box for donkey's years. In those days though you used to have to really work at using different names for passports, but now if it's got a British or EU cover they don't even check your passport. Interpol has got files on most of the big boys, so they used to just go and do the job under a different name. Now it's hardly worth the bother organising a false passport, unless you are going out of Europe. Jimmy O'Shaughnessy went to considerably more effort and expense than he really needed when he escaped to France.

At the Bank of America trial on 15th June 1976, counsel for the prosecution said that bundles of notes with consecutive serial numbers stolen in the raid had been found buried in a wood near Brenchley in Kent, and also found in a suitcase in a flat in Kingston upon Thames. As we know, the money found in the wood was part of Banner's stash hidden for him by his friend 'Tag' Garthwaite, amounting to some £68,000 in money and jewellery.

Garthwaite himself was charged with receiving £32,810, which together with Banner's amount comes to £100,000, and so may well have come from Banner's share. He was also charged with receiving US$25,600 and some jewellery. Presumably this also came in the first place from or through Banner.

Stewart Banner has dropped out of sight, for the good of his health, after completing less than three years in jail on section 43, that is isolated from the other prisoners to save him from retribution. He was released early in 1978. Nevertheless he was beaten up a few times whilst serving his sentence. He now lives under an assumed identity.

The money found in the flat referred to in the trial, was part of O'Loughlin's whack. Jimmy involuntarily 'returned' £75,000 of his whack before going on the run, when the police found this in his old flat in Harroby Road, London, W1.

Jimmy, was sent to 'D' wing the top security wing of Wormwood Scrubs prison, just north of Acton in London. Later he was transferred to the much more modern top security prison, Long Lartin. In 1985 he was released. By then cocaine and other drug related crime had largely replaced robbery as the number one earner: it was the new game in town. Jimmy was interested.

On December 1986 Jimmy and Mickey West went on trial at Southwark Crown court for possessing two kilograms of cocaine in the previous year with intent to supply. Neither gave evidence, but their defense was that they had been asked by the police to set up a Colombian cocaine dealer.

Whilst on remand at O'Loughlin was caught in possession of a tiny radio microphone transmitter, which he hoped to use in the Marylebone Magistrates court next day in conjunction with his girlfriend who was parked a short distance away with recording equipment.

They were acquitted because of confusion by the police and bungled tape evidence. In fact the police were involved in the buy of two kilos of cocaine, and had actually authorised a £64,000 payment for the purchase. The eventual sting was meant to be for a much larger quantity of eighty kilos, or about £2.5 million wholesale, worth tens of millions on the street.

I know that Willy Gavroche handed back £125,000, and I know he's out and about now, but he makes out that he's virtually skint, and has nothing left from the job. It was rumoured that he had in fact 'handed back' closer to £500,000, but if he did then some of that probably fell into the wrong hands.

Jeffrey Houdan, whose place in Brixton had been used to further divide the loot, handed back £32,000, and was found guilty of receiving the token amount of £1,862 plus US$4,981 and some jewellery. Jeffrey Stitcher, Johnny's greengrocer friend had to give back £2,500 and one Krugerrand. Although these were 'specimen' amounts, their relative smallness indicates that most of the cash from this quarter made its way to safer havens.

Amongst the main team members, it was typical of Johnny to go running to different people to put some of the money into businesses for him. That's very risky because people lose money in businesses, even in good times. I know that Johnny's money was passed to several people to look after.

Tonka, one of Johnny's minders from Ponder's End, not far from where Johnny lived, bought a car lot with some of the money. Johnny put another lot of money into somebody else's hands who bought a snooker hall in Lewisham. Whether they still own the snooker hall now, I don't know. I know for a fact that Johnny didn't get anything out of the car front, because the bloke he put into it, Tonka, was the sort of bloke who would turn round and say, 'Johnny, the car game has gone so downhill, I've got nothing in the kitty any more,' instead of saying I've been putting it away on every deal, which he should have done. Johnny's that easy going, he'll accept it.

Johnny got 23 years reduced to 20 years. In fact Johnny did a bit more that 2/3rds of that. With his knowledge of locks an attempted escape was always on the cards. It's a long time to be inside, especially if you look around you and see what's been built up in the last 15 years in the meantime. Besides, the physical form of the currency has changed several times since then, and the original cash would no longer be legal tender. However the jewellery would probably, packed as it was in plastic, have been quite safe underground all these years.

I saw Johnny two days after the job, then I didn't see him for a while, until I helped him raise the money for his defense. Visiting privileges were doled out as tightly as a gnat's arse, so not being a relative I didn't go to see him. Maybe in the end it would have been simpler for him to plead guilty, and get a slightly lower sentence.

Since that day when he got out, and I gave him a lift up to London, Johnny hasn't been to see by anyone from the old gang. He saw his minders, closed what was left of his investments, sold up his shops, and disappeared. His wife, Viv, has long since moved in with a succession of other villains, and now lives quietly in South London with a retired villain. Johnny bears her no grudge. Since he got out, nobody knows where he's gone. If he's got any sense, he won't tell anybody either. I don't blame him. Only Johnny, his fence, and perhaps one of his minders knows exactly where the jewellery went. Some of it re-entered the market shortly after he was released.

To understand what happened to a lot of the gold from the Bank of America, it is important to realise that Charlie Wilson, the Great Train Robber, and Johnny Wilde were good friends. Don't forget that Johnny bought almost all the jewellery and a lot of the gold from the others on the Bank of America raid. Johnny was a friend of both Charlie Wilson and Roy Jimmy, who was on the Great Train Robbery as well. Johnny even made the keys for the Aylesbury Prison break attempt by other Great Train Robbers including Ronnie Biggs.

After being convicted for his part in the Great Train Robbery, Charlie Wilson escaped from Winson Green Prison, near Birmingham. Charlie never seems to have done a day's work in his life, and he has always had something on the boil. He eventually retired to Spain where he too got involved in the drug game, along with Gordon Goody, another of the Great Train Robbers. Through his involvement with the drug barons, Charlie got killed in 1990.

Whatever he did, he liked it to be big, so it comes as no surprise that Charlie Wilson started the infamous VAT fraud on Krugerrands. This took advantage of a godsend situation provided by Mrs. Thatcher when she declared that Krugerrands were not currency, and therefore must have VAT levied on them in the UK. The plan was to buy them VAT free in Jersey. They were then shipped to London to be sold. At one time Charlie was flying in from Jersey sometimes as many as one flight per day. When they were sold through the gold market in London, VAT was charged, but this was never declared back to the Customs and Excise, it was simply pocketed, or more likely ploughed back into more purchases.

Charlie may originally have got the idea about the Krugerrands from helping Johnny dispose of some of his coins from the Bank of America. It would have been no easy matter to sell large quantities of Krugerrands through a broker by just walking in off the street, without a plausible story as to where they originated from. Charlie supplied so many Krugerrands, that a few more from Johnny's stash would not have been noticed. Let's assume that Charlie got all the initial Krugerrands from Johnny, and using these built up a trade with a broker that was a bit iffy.

Once the broker could see that he had access to a large number of Krugerrands, Charlie said, 'If I can have bank credit I can get you as much as you like." This fella was a bit skeptical. Charlie went and got some more Krugerrands from the stash and took it to this fella. Soon the broker was extending him a hundred grand worth of credit, on the security of the initial Krugerrands, so he can go and buy more Krugerrands at a good price.

With this kind of bank credit they could now go to a gold wholesaler in Jersey and buy quantities at a good VAT-free wholesale price. But they needed the initial stash of Krugerrands to pump prime the deal and give the broker the necessary confidence to provide a bank credit. It was very simple, very clever how they did it.

By the end they were moving a lot of money. Later when they had disposed of Johnny's Krugerrands and could see the VAT profit potential, they simply started. importing them without paying VAT at the border, or in the case of Jersey there was really no border.

I've got a feeling it was the broker that ended up putting Charlie away, because Charlie ended up taking the broker for a nice few quid. When I say a nice few quid, I mean half a million, three quarters, or more. Charlie just couldn't resist putting one over on the broker using a bank and telephone scam. But he shouldn't have done it, because that caused the broker to report the whole thing to the cozzers.

I want to tell you something now, it was a strict confidence told to me by a certain Old Bill. The order to nick Charlie is rumoured to have come from Margaret Thatcher herself, because she was so annoyed that someone was making a successful job of free enterprise out of her ridiculous change in the law. It was thought that he was getting away with too much, and making a mockery of the VAT, so they had to get him.

They did nick him and just to make sure, they planted on him a blueprint. I know that when they tried to nick him, instead of trying to do him cleverly, Old Bill tried to say he had with him the plans of the route of a security van that they were going to hit. He didn't have it. They planted it on him. He tore them to pieces in court. His record showed that he'd never done that sort of thing, physically he wasn't that sort of armed robber. Eventually when the full details of the VAT fraud were discovered, Charlie handed back some four hundred thousand pounds, but he still made a tidy profit. That is how a lot of the Bank of America coins got back into circulation.

He was a big man Charlie. He was a very clever person, but he was an unassuming sort of person. In the respect that he was well respected but nobody really knew what he was about all the time. He had his finger in so many little pies.

Mickey Jevons was also clever, as well as being a robber he was an international conmen. He used to go abroad with a mate and work a flim flam routine that they're good at between them.

Mickey Jevons went on to greater things, and continued to make history as a major league robber. He was involved in the Silver Bullion job with Lennie Gibson. For this Mickey dressed up as policemen and stopped a bullion lorry, unprotected and carrying about £3.5 million pounds in silver, owned by the government of East Germany. With accomplices he drove the silver to a north London lockup, but was not able to figure out how to cash the prize.

After a tip-off the police later found it all except for twelve bars in a lockup at North London. After being grassed himself, Mickey Jevons turned supergrass, and was responsible for the jailing of his partner on the Silver Bullion job. He claimed, and was even suing the police for, the standard 10% or £340,000 reward money which was offered by the loss adjusters for the Silver Bullion job. He actually was going to profit from the reward, but there was some confusion as to who deserved it. The reward is believed to instead have gone to Dave Ranger. Mickey was not short of a bob or two, but he just could not give up the buzz he got from doing just one more mega heist. An air of police corruption also surrounded the supergrass system and DI Tony Lundy who convinced Mickey to become a supergrass.

People like Mickey Jevons who are successful, they've got so much money that they have accumulated, that they don't only rob for the money at times, it becomes a buzz, as much as anything else. The challenge is to do it, and then to organise themselves all the way down the line, including the spiriting away of the money. If they get nicked they say, 'Well I didn't do it, did I? Prove it, where's the money? If I did it, where is the money?" and that sort of thing.

Sometimes the money is left, like the silver from the Silver Bullion job, in just a lockup, under railway arches somewhere. Thieves seem to be very casual about their own security. I went to a garage the other day that only had one lock on it. It was full bottom to top with stuff.

Freddie Maiser no, he didn't get captured. But its common knowledge that he was in on it — certainly to Old Bill. I don't know the other two who were lookouts. Freddie Maiser got away, ungrassed, probably because he had dangerous connections, and also because he was not known to many people on the job, and was not involved in the first attempt. The cozzers pulled Freddie in eventually in 1981, as part of Operation Carter. When they did eventually do him they raided his house but they couldn't initially get in. Freddie had a steel bar running right the way through the door and into the wall, so it couldn't be broken into. Eventually they went round the back and got in anyway.

They found twenty two diamonds hidden in Freddie's chimney breast. He had one diamond from the Bank of America job, the size of a hen's egg out of there. That one diamond he didn't get nicked for, because he had had it cut up. It would definitely have been recognisable and perhaps traceable otherwise. Freddie was like Johnny, he always had money.

He was successful at what he's done from a financial point of view, but luck doesn't last forever. In June 1981 he and George Copley came up for trial at Oxford on robbery charges, as a result of Operation Carter. A tape was produced with a record of a conversation between a cozzer and Copley implying police corruption. The case was thrown out of court. But the police do not forget such events, and after another robbery trial he was convicted, and he is now doing a 15 year stretch for armed robbery.

In March 1989 Dave Ranger, who discussed fencing the bulk of the jewellery from the Bank of America raid with Johnny Wilde before the raid, and who might well have been responsible for the pre-raid grassing, was accused at the Old Bailey of smuggling the largest known consignment of cocaine into Britain. He was arrested by Customs and Excise officers, over which his contacts at Scotland Yard had no control. His old friend and contact in the police force DI Tony Lundy had hastily retired from the police on the grounds of 'ill health' a short time before, still in his mid-forties. Despite a special plea by Lundy, who came out of retirement just for this purpose, Ranger was found guilty and jailed for 22 years. It is ironic that his sentence very nearly equaled Johnny's in length.

In December 1978, the Bank of America decided that the robbery occurred because of poor security, and issued a writ against Group 4 Total Security of Broadway Worcester, claiming considerable damages for negligence and the breaking of their agreement in providing adequate security services to the bank. By June 1993, the Bank had closed its Mayfair office altogether, and concentrated on doing business solely in the City of London. Small branches of foreign banks had gone out of fashion in Mayfair some time before. Besides, competitors in the safe deposit business had sprung up in other parts of Mayfair, including one just a block away in Davies Street.

What happened to the rest of the money? Over £25 million. That is a tale for another time.

GLOSSARY OF SLANG TERMS

apple core	score, 20 pounds
architect	the person who plans out the detail of a 'job' right down to the timings and routes
bad news	gun
bang	gelignite
banged up	jailed, locked up
bang to rights	caught red handed
battle cruiser	boozer, pub, bar
bellman	the man whose job it is to disable the alarms before a burglary
bird	'doing bird', doing a prison sentence. Australian slang for a woman or girl
bit of work	a crooked job
blag/blagging	robbery
blinding	brilliant
boozer	pub or drinking club
bottle	courage
bottley	afraid, scared
bull's eye	50 pounds (as in darts)
bust	a police raid
busted	arrested
cane	to open with crowbars or jemmies
catchers	criminals. Top catchers were prominent criminals, worthy of respect by the fraternity
Charlie Bananas	acting the cocky show-off
cock & hen	ten pounds
cozzer	policeman
dets	detonators, used by safe crackers
dog-eye	lookout

drink	a fee paid to someone doing a minor part, or providing an auxiliary service for a job, such as stealing cars to order
drum	house or home
flop	see slaughter
faces	known criminals
fitted up	wrongly accused or convicted on the basis of spurious evidence often provided by the police
fraternity	the boys, the criminal fraternity
gear	stolen property
gelly	gelignite, as used by safe crackers
grand	1000 pounds
grass	someone who supplies the police with information about criminal activities (sometimes supposed to come from the Inkspots greatest hit 'Whispering Grass')
grassed up	betrayed to the police
groins	finger rings
hambone	phone
horse	heroin
jar up	a scam with jewellery, where worthless rings replace genuine items just before the sale
job	a robbery or other criminal activity
jump ups	armed robberies
kettle	watch
keyman	key and lock specialist, who would provide copy or skeleton keys for burglaries
kite	cheque
lively	criminally active, regularly doing 'jobs'
lolly	money
moody	bent or illegal or tarted up

Old Bill	the police
peter	safe
piece of work	plan for a robbery or an offer of a crooked job
pony	25 pounds
porridge	time in jail
prize	a specific objective that a thief sets out to steal
Rosy Lee	tea
rozzer	policeman
ruck	fight
Rule 43	the rule that allows a prisoner to be kept in solitary confinement for his own protection from other prisoners, often used for grasses
score	to collect, the payout, especially in a drugs purchase.
sent down	convicted
shooters	guns
skint	broke
screws	prison warders
slaughter	the place where the spoils of a robbery are divided
snow	cocaine
speed	methedrine or dexedrine, often taken before a job to speed up the reflexes
spin	search by the police
stash	secret hoard of stolen money, or jewellery
Sweeney Todd	Flying Squad
stick together	organise, specifically a 'job'
tasty	handy, able to defend himself
Thursday Mob	a bank robbing gang which got its name from the day of the week they used to strike

tickles	criminal jobs, specifically confidence tricks
tom	jewellery
turtled up	wearing gloves
turtles	gloves
twirls	keys
whack	An equal share of the proceeds of a job, as opposed to a 'drink', a fixed fee

APPENDIX

LEAGUE TABLE OF UK ROBBERIES

Date	Robbery	Amount	In 2016 values
1963	Great Train Robbery	£ 2.6 m	£ 49 million
1971	Lloyds Baker Street	£ 3.0 m	£ 38 million
1975	Bank of America	£26.0 m	£ 197 million
1983	Brinks Mat	£26.3 m	£ 80 million
1987	Knightsbridge Safe Deposit	£40 m	£ 101 million

Made in the USA
Columbia, SC
05 November 2018